ALLEN COUNTY PUBLIC LIBRARY

3 1833 02

S0-BWS-987

Fiction
Gray, Juliet.
The crystal cage

SPECIAL MESSAGE TO READERS

This book is published under the auspices of
THE ULVERSCROFT FOUNDATION
(registered charity No. 264873 UK)

Established in 1972 to provide funds for
research, diagnosis and treatment of eye diseases.
Examples of contributions made are: —

A new Children's Assessment Unit at
Moorfield's Hospital, London.

Twin operating theatres at the
Western Ophthalmic Hospital, London.

A Chair of Ophthalmology at the
University of Leicester.

The establishment of a Royal Australian College
of Ophthalmologists "Fellowship".

You can help further the work of the Foundation
by making a donation or leaving a legacy. Every
contribution, no matter how small, is received
with gratitude. Please write for details to:

**THE ULVERSCROFT FOUNDATION,
The Green, Bradgate Road, Anstey,
Leicester LE7 7FU, England.
Telephone: (0116) 236 4325**

In Australia write to:
**THE ULVERSCROFT FOUNDATION,
c/o The Royal Australian College of
Ophthalmologists,
27, Commonwealth Street, Sydney,
N.S.W. 2010.**

THE CRYSTAL CAGE

Jessica's adoration of the man she had married seemed to imprison her in a crystal cage. Trapped by her dependence on the handsome actor who moulded her into the kind of wife he wanted, she could see what she needed for her happiness but could not reach out for it. When Ritchie desired another woman, Jessica found herself with a freedom she did not know how to use. Her loving heart needed a new and lasting home — but who would supply it?

Books by Juliet Gray
in the Linford Romance Library:

WHEN FORTUNE SMILES
BID ME LOVE
ALWAYS IS FOR EVER
THE COST OF LOVING
A HEART FOR HEALING
THIS IS MY DESTINY
SWEET REBEL
SHADOW ON A STAR
RAINBOW GOLD
ARROW OF DESIRE

JULIET GRAY

THE CRYSTAL CAGE

Complete and Unabridged

LINFORD
Leicester

First published in Great Britain

Allen County Public Library
900 Webster Street
PO Box 2270
Fort Wayne, IN 46801-2270

First Linford Edition
published 1996

Copyright © 1974 by Juliet Gray
All rights reserved

British Library CIP Data

Gray, Juliet, *1933 –*
    The crystal cage.—Large print ed.—
Linford romance library
1. English fiction—20th century
I. Title
823.9′14 [F]

ISBN 0–7089–7924–6

Published by
F. A. Thorpe (Publishing) Ltd.
Anstey, Leicestershire

Set by Words & Graphics Ltd.
Anstey, Leicestershire
Printed and bound in Great Britain by
T. J. Press (Padstow) Ltd., Padstow, Cornwall

This book is printed on acid-free paper

1

THE night was deepening and Jessica's taut, overstrung nerves seemed to relax just a little of their tension as she drove slowly through the unfamiliar countryside. The twin headlights of her car threw the tall hedges and overhanging trees into stark relief against the darkening sky. She was less than forty miles from London yet the quiet and velvety peace of her surroundings were exactly what she needed. She was desperate for sanctuary, a place to hide her heartache, the cool shadows after the dazzling limelight of unpleasant and unwelcome publicity.

Following instructions, she had left the arterial road some miles distant. The lane was narrow and winding and she had counted only a handful of scattered properties as she drove deeper into the heart of the country. Hester had warned her that the cottage was off the beaten track and might not be easy to find. Perfect for her needs, Jessica thought miles from anywhere and with very little likelihood of being sniffed out by those reporters whose one aim in life seemed just then to be the dissection of her private affairs.

It was odd that Hester, who was not really a close friend, should have known so well what she needed. Other friends had urged her to forget in a wild pursuit of pleasure, had recommended Paris, New York, Monaco, Bermuda, had showered her with invitations and expressed horror at her quiet insistence that she wanted some place where she could be utterly alone to lick her wounds. Hester had understood. She had quietly offered the cottage for as long as she wished to use it and assured her that wild horses would not persuade her to part with the address.

Utterly weary and dispirited, Jessica had seized the opportunity to escape

. . . and if her sudden disappearance evoked another furore of publicity at least she would not be within easy reach at the end of a telephone line or have to endure the humiliation of seeing her own name and face blazoned across the front pages of the daily papers.

The winding road seemed to be endless. Idly she wondered if she had lost her way. It was a novel experience to realize that it would not matter if she spent the entire night driving aimlessly about the countryside. For there was no one waiting at journey's end and no one to answer to but herself. This was freedom, she supposed . . . the one luxury she had been denied for so long. Freedom to please herself, to go where she wished, to do what she wanted, to be her own mistress. Ritchie had given her something really worth the having at last, she thought wryly . . .

Abruptly she shied from the thought of him. She had gained freedom, perhaps, but she had lost everything else that she had valued and cherished. The ache had seemed to subside a little as she drew further away from London with all its unhappy associations but it suddenly swelled anew to anguish — and at that moment she thankfully saw a signpost in the glare of the headlights.

Bednoken 3 miles. The cottage must be close now if she had correctly remembered Hester's hasty instructions. She slowed the car, scanned the seemingly unbroken line of hedgerow on both sides of the lane. Then she saw it . . . the narrow, rutted lane leading to the left with a scarcely distinguishable nameboard leaning drunkenly against the hedge.

She followed the ruts of Redvers Cut for some distance before she saw the cottage. She was surprised, having expected something smaller and much more primitive. Then, thinking of the elegant and sophisticated Hester, she realized that the misnomer of 'country cottage' was understandable.

She drove through the open gate and towards the gabled house. Hester had mentioned the garage but failed to warn her that the doors would slide up and out of sight with silent, automatic efficiency at the car's approach. Jessica smiled faintly . . . not so primitive, certainly. It was evident that Hester had installed every mod. con.

It was something of a setback to discover that she could not open the front door. The key slipped easily enough into the lock but simply would not turn. Jessica wondered if Hester had given her the wrong key . . . easy enough in the rush. Perhaps the lock was just stiff through little use — after all, Hester had warned her that the cottage hadn't been used for some time and might be rather dusty and cold.

She made her way round to the back, feeling that she was perfectly within her rights to force an entrance if necessary and determined that she was not going to turn back now. The garden was very well-kept and she supposed that Hester must employ one of the local people to keep it in such good order.

There was an old-fashioned latch on the back door and she raised it rather tentatively. The door swung open. With an odd little twinge of guilt, she stepped across the threshold and found herself in a kitchen. There was still sufficient light for her to see that it was a large and very modern kitchen, beautifully planned and fitted, spotlessly clean and meticulously tidy. Hester had not explained the domestic arrangements but obviously she employed someone to keep the house in perfect readiness for occupation — which explained that swift offer to lend it to Jessica although she had not been down to the cottage for some time herself. Hester was a wealthy young woman and it would not bother her unduly to lay out such expense on the mere chance that she or her friends might wish to use the cottage.

Jessica explored further in surprise

and delight. Hester had certainly understated the case, she decided with a flicker of amusement. The 'cottage' was a lovely little house, modernized by experts and sparing no expense to provide it with every comfort and convenience.

It was a quiet, welcoming house and Jessica had the oddest fancy that the cottage was waiting for the return of someone who had only left it briefly. For herself, she felt that she had come home . . . a feeling she had not known in any of the luxurious flats, houses, villas or hotel suites which she had shared with Ritchie during the past six years.

The tumult of her heart and mind seemed instantly quietened by the enveloping peace and friendliness of these surroundings. This was a home, she felt . . . a place to relax, to forget, to allow time to heal, to be herself again — the real Jessica Conrad. For so long she had been moulded to Ritchie's pattern . . . she had almost forgotten how to think and feel for herself. This house was evoking the first faint stirrings of independence . . . this dear little house that she already felt she would never want to leave. It was the sanctuary she sought and she blessed Hester for her timely generosity.

Knowing that she had plenty of time to acquaint herself thoroughly with the house, Jessica brought her cases from the car just as night really descended. She had also brought a box of provisions with her, having been warned that the nearest village shop was three or four miles from the cottage.

She rejected the largest of the bedrooms . . . the double bed did not please her with its reminder of the intimacies of married life. The smallest bedroom would suit her very well, she decided . . . and she liked the virginal white spread on the neat little bed. White and palest lavender . . . a delightful colour scheme for a charming room. The bed was made up — it seemed that Hester was determined that the place should be in absolute readiness for any impulsive decision on her part to use it.

Jessica unpacked only what she needed for the night, too weary to do more until morning. She had not paused to pack all her many lovely suits and dresses and shoes, the furs and wraps and evening gowns, thrusting into a couple of cases only what she needed for a brief absence from town. Later she must make arrangements to collect the rest of her clothes and personal possessions.

She changed out of the neat suit into a nightgown and a white velvet housecoat and thankfully released her heavy mass of hair from its pins, giving it a perfunctory brushing and allowing it to curl loosely about her slim shoulders. Then she went down to the kitchen. She had already discovered that the house was not only supplied with electricity but was also switched on at the main. She was grateful for the fact as she filled the electric kettle and plugged it in. She made tea and a sandwich and carried the snack meal into the comfortable sitting-room. An electric fire stood in the hearth and although she did not feel cold she switched it on for the comfort of its glowing coals.

After all, she was not hungry but she was grateful for the hot tea which she slowly sipped as she sat in the deep wing chair with bare feet stretched towards the glowing bars of the fire. It was a very pleasant room with its comfortable chairs and thick carpet. She pulled the heavy drapes across the wide floor-to-ceiling window that occupied the whole of one wall, shutting out the night which had abruptly become wild, wet and windy.

A magnificent portrait of Hester hung above the stone fireplace . . . Jessica admired it and wondered at the delicate skill of the artist who had captured Hester's fragile loveliness so well and yet managed to convey the inner strength and determination behind that seemingly vulnerable femininity.

A clock chimed softly — and Jessica felt a tiny shiver run down her spine. Surely it was a little eerie that the clock was not only going but also showing near enough the right time! Then she mocked herself . . . of course, it was an electric clock and hadn't she already discovered that everything in the house was ready for instant occupation? It was just another indication of that practical streak in Hester that surprised her friends. Obviously Hester had telephoned the person she employed to look after the place in order to give warning that a friend was borrowing the cottage and to ensure that the electricity was switched on, a duster put over each room and the beds made up in readiness. How stupid not to have thought of that before, Jessica chided herself.

She relaxed again in her chair, warm and comfortable and a little drowsy . . . she was almost asleep but she could not make the effort to get up out of the chair and make her way up the narrow stairs to the bed that waited for her . . .

Curled up in the chair, her cheek cradled on her hand, Jessica slept like a child — and did not know how much later it was when she woke. She was not sure what had woken her and it was a few seconds before she could associate an oddly familiar little sound with its significance — and just as she realized that it had been the sound of a key turning in a lock, a man appeared in the open doorway of the room . . .

He was very tall, very broad . . . a mountain of a man. A very handsome man in a dark dinner suit and gleaming white linen. His hair was burnished gold, blazing in the lamplight, and his eyes were incredibly blue and commanding . . . and widening now with astonishment at the sight of Jessica.

She stared at him blankly, incredulously . . . So shocked that she could neither move nor speak, frozen in her chair, her heart seemingly stopped in that moment as alarm tingled in her veins. Her mind was still clouded with sleep and she could only regard the man as an intruder who meant ill . . . quite failing to read the significance in his possession of a key to the house, his air of easy familiarity with his surroundings and his obvious astonishment and swift suspicion of her presence.

Returning from an evening spent with friends, Gavin had not been surprised to find a car already occupying the garage. The gleam of the lamp betrayed that the house was not empty and he had very naturally assumed that his sister was home earlier than expected. Hurrying into the house in eager anticipation of finding Rosa, he had been instantly checked in his stride at the sight of a complete stranger.

Perhaps he was tired. Perhaps he had drunk just a little too much of Clive's excellent brandy. Usually the most quick-witted of men, he leaped foolishly to the conclusion that he was being hounded again by one of those stupid young sensation-seekers who sought to involve a famous name in a scandal. It was not the first time a woman had cast out lures but this was carrying things a little too far, he thought in very natural anger at the invasion of his privacy.

"What the devil are you doing here?" he demanded roughly.

Jessica rose to her feet, taut and wary. "I might ask you the same thing," she returned stiffly, facing him courageously but feeling extremely weak about the knees. She glanced instinctively about for some means of defence if this tall and very muscular man should take one step towards her. "What do you want?" she challenged him bravely.

Gavin stared in surprise. "I'm asking the questions," he told her curtly. "Unless you prefer to explain yourself to the local constable?"

Her eyes widened. "What do you mean . . . ?" she gasped in bewilderment, doubting the accuracy of her ears.

Gavin was checked by the bewilderment in her tone, the confusion in her grey eyes. She seemed genuinely astonished that he should resent her presence, he thought drily . . . she must be a very accomplished actress. But he was in no mood to play the part she had obviously chosen for him . . . despite the charm and the loveliness that belatedly caught his attention.

His glance raked her from head to foot, taking in the slender body beneath the heavy, luxurious robe, the crisp curling mass of hair that tumbled about her shoulders, the perfect oval of a lovely face with its small, shapely nose and tremulous mouth, the wide-eyed innocence of expression . . . and certainly her eyes were very striking, he decided with a quickening of artistic appreciation.

With an effort he dragged his mind back to the matter in hand. "I mean that I won't tolerate this kind of thing," he said grimly.

Jessica looked at him blankly. "I don't understand . . . "

"You seem to have made yourself very much at home," he cut in drily. "I think I'm entitled to some explanation, don't you?"

"There has been some mistake," Jessica said slowly, confused. "I don't know what you are talking about!"

"The mistake is yours, believe me," he told her coldly and with contempt. "You have laid on a very cosy homecoming but you have wasted your time, I'm afraid."

Jessica wrinkled her brow in the effort to concentrate on the words and their implications. Perhaps it was the strain of recent days, the nervous exhaustion which threatened to overwhelm her or simply the shock of his sudden appearance but she seemed quite unable to make any sense of the situation.

The blood drained suddenly from her cheeks and a strange coldness filled her veins as the room began to whirl about her . . . blindly, instinctively she put out a hand to him and cried in panic: "Please . . . I think . . . I'm going . . . "

Gavin caught the slight body in his arms as she crumpled, highly suspicious of that convenient faint. But he swiftly realized that it was not pretence as she lay a dead weight against him. He swung her up into his arms and carried her across the room to a couch. Baffled, bewildered, he set her down and smoothed the tumbled hair from that lovely face. He looked down at her for a moment, frowning . . . and then he went to pour a glass of brandy.

Jessica came slowly out of the faint, too bemused to realize where she was or what had happened until she knew the pungent taste of brandy on her lips. She choked and swiftly averted her face, disliking the very smell of the spirit.

"A little more," Gavin said quietly but firmly, his hand beneath her head as he raised her slightly from the cushions.

It was useless to protest, she realized. Hating it, she obediently took another sip and tried not to choke on it . . . then she struggled to sit up, to push away the hand that held the glass.

"All right . . . I won't make you drink any more of it," he assured her gently, setting down the glass. "But don't try to get up just yet . . . you still look very pale."

There was an authority in his voice that she instinctively obeyed. She sank back against the cushions and looked up at him with mixed feelings. It was impossible not to be grateful for his ministrations and certainly there was nothing to alarm her in the impersonal air with which he regarded her, standing by the couch and looking down at her from his great height. She felt ridiculously small and helpless but not at all frightened of him any longer, having sensed the innate kindliness with which he had tended her just as he might care for a hurt child or

18

an injured animal, she thought a little incoherently.

"Thank you . . . I'm grateful," she said stiffly. "Fainting isn't — usually one of my pastimes . . . but you frightened me, you know."

He raised an eyebrow . . . a cynical little gesture. "You must forgive me," he said drily. "But a man has the right to enter his own home, surely."

She sat up quickly . . . almost too quickly as her head swam briefly but cleared again. She looked at him with unmistakable astonishment in her grey eyes — and he looked back at her in swift revision of his earlier suspicions . . .

2

"**T**HIS is . . . *your* house?" Jessica asked slowly. "Is that what you are saying?"

"You didn't know that, of course," he mocked her but not unkindly. "You were merely looking for somewhere to rest your weary head and are in the habit of breaking into other people's houses, no doubt."

Jessica caught her underlip between her teeth in dismay . . . the realization that this was not Hester's cottage had finally made its impact on her muddled mind. "So that's why the key wouldn't open the front door," she said bleakly.

Gavin frowned. "The key . . . "

She scarcely heard him. She was struggling with the appalling realization that she was the intruder, after all . . . "So stupid to suppose the house could have been standing empty for any length of time . . . so obviously lived in," she murmured, more to herself than to the man who studied her with narrowed eyes. "If I hadn't been so tired, so introspective . . . " She broke off, looking up at him ruefully. "I owe you an apology, it seems. For it does appear to be my mistake-and a very stupid one, I'm afraid. Tell me, is there another house in the near vicinity?"

Following the trend of her thoughts, he instinctively rejected the suggestion as much too unlikely . . . and all his suspicions returned despite the dismay that seemed so genuine. He had allowed himself to be briefly conned by the apparent frankness in those clear grey eyes, he told himself drily.

"There is a small cottage further down the lane," he admitted.

Jessica sighed. "And this isn't Brook Cottage," she said wryly.

His eyes hardened abruptly. For that was just too much for him to swallow . . . that anyone could confuse his well-kept and well-ordered home with a

21

poky little cottage that had never been completely modernized because Hester had lost interest in it after quarrelling with him.

"This is Redvers House," he told her coldly.

"Then I'm guilty of trespassing on your property at the very least . . . and I really don't know what to say," Jessica said and her voice shook slightly.

She swung her legs to the floor and rose a little unsteadily to her feet . . . and Gavin despite his annoyance and contempt, instinctively put a hand to her elbow and regarded her with just a hint of anxiety in his very blue eyes.

Suddenly she laughed. It was a choice between laughter and tears . . . and it was impossible for Jessica Conrad to give way to tears in the presence of a stranger. It was all so absurd, so ridiculous — and so heartbreakingly disappointing. The final straw . . .

She had fallen headlong in love with this house and felt that she must find a measure of contentment beneath its roof . . . but she had been trespassing from the very moment that she drove through the open gateway. How blind she had been, how foolish, how stupidly swift to assume that this charming and well-equipped house with its many overt indications of current occupation must be the cottage that Hester had offered as a temporary refuge.

This man had every right to be furious, indeed — and yet surely he could appreciate that there was a grain of humour in the situation?

Meeting his blue eyes, she met only a cold, cynical contempt in their depths . . . and abruptly she buried her face in her hands.

Gavin studied her, faint uncertainty dawning in his eyes. Was it all an act, part of a carefully laid plan . . . or was she really here by accident? It did not seem very likely but strange things could and did happen in life.

He suddenly felt that he needed a drink. It had been slightly disturbing to find a strange woman curled up in his armchair. It might be wise to give her another glass of brandy, too . . . her slim shoulders were heaving with suppressed sobs and he recognized the signs of severe emotional strain.

He strode to the cabinet. Glancing over his shoulder, he found that his unexpected guest was still struggling with her emotions. His eyes softened slightly for in that moment she looked like a vulnerable child rather than the calculating young woman he had supposed her to be.

If they were both victims of a genuine mistake then he could appreciate and understand her dismay. He liked to believe that he was a reasonably good judge of character and he found it difficult to reconcile the candour in those lovely eyes with the conviction that she had deliberately broken into his house to set a trap for him.

Wryly assuring himself that his tender heart would eventually cost him dear, he poured a little brandy into a glass and took it to the girl who seemed to be suddenly unaware of him, staring blindly into the distance. He touched her shoulder and she jerked from his hand. Women did not usually shrink from his touch and Gavin was illogically offended that this woman should instinctively recoil from him. But he swiftly reminded himself that they were strangers to each other . . . and she might not find it easy to trust any man.

Jessica looked blankly at the glass in his hand. Then she pulled herself together and managed a stiff little smile. "No, thank you . . . I seem to be making a fool of myself tonight but I really don't want that," she said bravely.

Gavin reached for cigarettes. Jessica hesitated when he offered the box and then she took one, leaning forward to accept a light. She rarely smoked . . . Ritchie did not approve of the habit in women. But it was no longer necessary or desirable to please

Ritchie — and she was grateful for the cooling, soothing nicotine for her jangled nerves.

She was beginning to regain a little of her self-possession but she was still very conscious of the awkwardness of the situation.

Gavin studied her, noting the tension in that slim body, the nervous fretting of the cigarette between slender fingers . . . and his eyes narrowed as he noticed the wide band of a wedding ring. She looked very young and rather forlorn as she stared at the glowing bar of the electric fire and he realized that momentarily her thoughts were far from him or her surroundings. She was in some sort of trouble, he decided . . .

Slowly Jessica became aware of him once more, aware of that steady gaze. She turned her head to look at him and found a compassion in the blue eyes that startled her. He had no reason to feel kindly towards her, after all . . . her presence in his house must seem very odd and very suspicious and she had not yet offered an adequate explanation for it.

Gavin's eyes crinkled slightly as he smiled. It was a smile that underlined the forceful attraction of his good looks . . . the smile that had charmed and encouraged many women. "Welcome back," he said lightly. "I thought you'd forgotten my existence."

She frowned faintly. "That isn't easy in the circumstances."

"But I don't know the circumstances," he reminded her drily, rebuffed by that curt response to a tentative overture of friendship.

"I feel terrible about the whole thing," she said impulsively. "But it's partly your fault, you know . . . if the back door had been locked I'd have gone away assuming that Hester had given me the wrong key."

Gavin glanced at the large portrait that dominated the room. "Ah . . . Hester," he said slowly, inclined to distrust on principle anyone who claimed friendship with that particular woman.

"If you are one of Hester's friends then that explains a great deal."

Jessica wondered if she only imagined the grimness of his tone. "So are you, it seems," she said lightly, indicating the portrait with a faint smile and wondering with feminine curiosity why it held such pride of place in this man's house.

"We were neighbours at one time," he said smoothly. "But you know that, of course."

"I do now," she agreed wryly. "But I was trying to explain . . . Hester offered me the cottage to use for as long as I like and I was very pleased to accept. My . . . my reasons wouldn't interest you," she added abruptly although he had not indicated the slightest curiosity.

"And did she tell you how long it is since she used it herself?" he asked drily.

"She said it was some months."

"Several winter months. The place must be very cold and damp and unpleasant. I should hesitate to offer it to anyone before I'd opened it up and made it fit for human habitation. Dear, impulsive Hester . . . " he added mockingly.

"Oh dear . . . is it so very bad?" Jessica asked anxiously.

"Well, it isn't Redvers House," he told her with a faintly sardonic inflection.

"I couldn't know that," she said defensively.

"Being a stranger in these parts?" he mocked gently.

Her chin tilted. "That's true . . . I don't know this area at all. I've never seen the cottage and it just didn't occur to me that this wasn't Hester's place. Oh, I was surprised to find it so well-kept, of course — but it was easy to assume that she employed someone to look after it." Her eyes held a defiant challenge as they met the cynical amusement in his gaze. "That's perfectly feasible!" she exclaimed sharply.

"Even to the extent of keeping the larder stocked with fresh food?" he asked idly, nodding at the tray with its empty cup and untouched sandwich.

Her eyes flashed with sudden indignation. "I don't know about that — I didn't investigate! I brought supplies with me, naturally. I may be an unwitting trespasser but there's no need to treat me like a common criminal. I know the whole business is quite farcical but I really haven't harmed your precious property!" She rose to her feet and stalked towards the door with as much dignity as she could muster. "I'll remove myself as soon as possible!"

Gavin looked at her with amusement glinting in his eyes . . . and something more than amusement. In that moment he felt the first faint stirring of interest. So she had a temper to match that glorious red-gold hair . . . and he had the oddest conviction that she had thoroughly enjoyed ripping out at him. It was just as though she had been compelled to keep her tongue between her teeth for a very long time and it was a relief to speak her mind freely.

Suddenly, without rhyme or reason, he knew the identity of his unexpected guest . . . right out of the blue he could put a name to this lovely woman who had appeared so strangely beneath his roof.

In common with almost everyone, he knew of Ritchie Conrad . . . and he had particular cause to know of him although they had never met. Handsome, talented, supremely confident, he was a magnet to attract the admiration of most — and the willing compliance of any woman he chanced to want, thought Gavin with a sudden surging of renewed anger.

It was not surprising that he had failed to recognize Conrad's wife. She had been kept very much in the background, he fancied. He might have known her from the press photographs of recent days if he had been sufficiently interested in the daily tabloids and their delight in the sudden shattering of the Conrad marriage. But he did not follow the careers and affairs of the famous with the avidity that Imogen had displayed when she had surprised and rather bored him that evening by having all the facts of the Conrad upset at her finger-tips. All the published facts, he amended wryly, knowing very well that reporters occasionally suppressed some facts and invented others in the interest of good copy.

He scarcely knew why he was so sure that his visitor was Ritchie Conrad's wife . . . it was intuition rather than recognition. If she was telling the truth it was an odd circumstance that had brought her to his house. If she was lying he could not think of any motive she could have for intruding into his life.

Whatever the explanation for her presence he could not allow her to walk out into the wet and blustery night at this hour. He drawled carelessly: "Do you mean to spend a most

32

uncomfortable night at Brook Cottage? I couldn't have it on my conscience, you know. You'd be well advised to remain here."

Jessica turned to look at him, startled. "You can't be serious!"

He smiled, his eyes crinkling in that very attractive manner. "Why not? You are not concerned with the conventions, surely? It's a foul night and your car will probably get bogged down in the mud before you get to the cottage. Pride is all very well but it certainly takes second place to convenience at times, in my view."

His reasoning seemed sufficiently sound — in the circumstances. But she still hesitated. "I don't know . . . "

He shrugged. "Please yourself, of course," he said indifferently. "But I suspect that the cottage has a leak in the roof and you'll scarcely want to knock up the village pub at this hour — even if you could find it!"

Jessica glanced at the clock and was shaken to discover that it was well past midnight. She had not realized that it was so late. "I've caused you a lot of trouble already," she said uncertainly. "And we don't really know each other," she added lamely.

She wanted to stay . . . she shrank from the thought of dressing, repacking, going out into the wild night to find a cottage which did not sound at all inviting from his description. She ached with weariness and she longed for the promised comfort of that bed in the delightful room above her head. She ought not to stay, of course . . . it was not only unconventional to accept the hospitality of a total stranger. It could well be dangerous!

Yet she would not believe that she had any reason to fear him. There was nothing in his manner to alarm her and he was much too matter of fact, even indifferent. She reminded herself that they had a mutual friend in Hester . . . not really a very good justification for staying but at least a reassurance of sorts.

Gavin watched the changing expressions flit across that lovely face as the thoughts chased each other through her mind. He believed that he correctly construed most of them. Her indecision was intriguing. He fancied that she was a mixture of emotional impulse and sound practicality and he wondered which would win the obvious struggle.

"Will it help if I tell you my name? Or do you insist on character references?" His tone was gently teasing. "Of course, the very mention of my name might decide the matter for you . . . you see, I am Gavin Brice."

He uttered the famous name without pride or apology but it did not have the immediate impact that he had come to expect.

"Oh, are you . . . ?" She was unimpressed. "I thought there was something vaguely familiar about you . . . I suppose we must have met at some time. One of Hester's parties, perhaps?"

"It's possible," he agreed. "But I

don't think I should have forgotten if I had met you before."

She moved slightly, impatient with the obvious compliment. She glanced instinctively at the portrait above the fireplace, aware now that it was his work . . . and she could not help wondering if Hester had been one of his many conquests.

Gavin Brice was a brilliant artist. He was also reputed to make love to every woman who sat for him, claiming that he gained true insight into character and personality through such intimate association. Such stories about the famous were common and Jessica knew better than to believe half of them. After all, some of the things that had been said and written about Ritchie had been absolutely ludicrous . . .

He did not look like an unscrupulous rake, anyway . . . although good looks and easy manners and the kind of charm that inspired confidence must all be part of the stock-in-trade of a rake, she reminded herself.

36

Noting that swift glance, his lips quirked with laughter as he realized the trend of her thoughts. "My reputation is rather a bore," he said lightly. "One doesn't always care to live up to it."

Jessica regarded him steadily. "Is that a reassurance?" she asked bluntly.

"If you feel that you need one . . ."

She shook her head, smiling faintly. "I imagine the stories have been very much exaggerated. I don't suppose you've really seduced every woman you've painted."

An answering smile lurked at the corner of his mouth. "Because of the quantity, do you mean — or the quality?" he asked, his eyes twinkling.

"Both, I should suppose," she returned frankly.

He chuckled. "You are a very perceptive person," he said lightly.

Her face clouded abruptly. "No . . . you are mistaken," she said bitterly. "I'm one of those people who never see the obvious."

He understood the allusion and the

bitterness, so convinced was he of her identity. But, seeking confirmation, he said gently: "You haven't yet told me your name?"

"Oh! It's Con-Conway . . . Jessica Conway," she said, faltering a little but hoping he might not have noticed that hasty amendment. It was too much to hope that he would not be familiar with her real name or the publicity that had attached to it lately . . .

3

GAVIN looked across the room at her for a long moment. He appreciated her desire for anonymity but there was no point in pretence that would only lead to eventual embarrassment.

"Conrad, I think . . . " he said quietly.

Her hands clenched abruptly and she looked at him with sudden dislike. "You might have pretended to believe me!" she flared resentfully.

"I have no finesse," he admitted ruefully, smiling in warm understanding.

"Oh . . . what does it matter!" she exclaimed with little regard for the truth. "I don't know why I bothered to lie . . . one can't escape, obviously." She threw up her head and faced him, challenging him to delight as everyone else did in the humiliation that had been thrust upon her. "I suppose you know the whole story!"

"I only know what I've seen in the newspapers," Gavin returned carelessly. "I don't suppose that's the whole story, by any means . . . and I don't know that I'm very interested, you know. There's no novelty in a broken marriage these days."

His very indifference was oddly comforting, seeming to minimize the humiliation she had been feeling and encouraging her to wonder if it was foolish to suppose the whole world to be sneering because the Conrads had 'agreed to part' . . . a reporter's bland assessment of Ritchie's brutal declaration that he no longer wished to live with her!

Desolation suddenly engulfed her, sweeping aside the few grains of comfort she had found in this man's easy acceptance of the circumstances. She felt so utterly alone, knowing that there was nothing and no one who could help her to adjust to life without Ritchie. All her happiness, her security, her peace of mind had been whisked away without warning. The world would describe her agony and Ritchie's betrayal just as this man did . . . dismissing with light indifference all the hopes, all the dreams, all the desires that had gone into the making of a marriage . . .

Gavin could not bear to see the anguish that twisted her beautiful face so abruptly. He said sharply: "Don't wallow, woman! You're better off without him — and the sooner you come to terms with that truth the better you'll feel!"

She was immediately incensed. What right had a stranger to pass judgement on Ritchie . . . or to tell her that she was better off without a husband who could not be faithful? Her heart ceased to swell and her eyes to prickle with unshed tears. She glared at Gavin Brice, her temper rising. "I may be obliged to accept your hospitality but I certainly don't have to endure your comments on my personal affairs," she said coldly, haughtily . . . and immediately spoilt any effect she might have achieved by adding in a rather shaky voice: "And if I want to wallow I shall wallow, damn you!"

In that moment she struck a blow for her personal independence. For too many years she had submitted meekly to another person's dictums and wishes and she was quite determined to have a mind of her own in future and to follow her own inclinations at last.

Gavin smiled, pleased with the success of his strategy. "Quite right, too," he agreed smoothly, taking the wind out of her sails. "But in private, don't you think?"

"Oh! . . . Yes . . . yes, of course," she agreed, snatching at her composure and appreciating the timeliness of his reminder that one did not embarrass strangers with one's most intimate feelings.

"I gather you've decided to stay . . . very sensible of you," he went on carelessly. "Better to risk a reputation than pneumonia on a night like this — and no one need know that my sister was away, after all."

Surprise flickered in her eyes. "Your sister?"

"She lives with me," he explained lightly. "She's away at the moment, staying with friends. But I'm expecting her home at any time . . . indeed, I thought she was back when I saw the lights. As it happens, it works out very well for you may sleep in her room."

"I fancy I've already claimed it," Jessica said wryly. "That is . . . if it's the one directly above this room?"

"Yes. She wouldn't mind at all, I promise you," he assured her carelessly.

"Then I'll go up . . . if you don't mind," she said tentatively.

"You must be tired," he agreed. "You know your way, of course . . . I hope you sleep well."

"Thank you . . . you are very kind," she murmured shyly, feeling the words were wholly inadequate to express what she really felt at being granted a few more hours of the security she found within these walls . . .

Gavin poured himself a final drink, a faint frown touching his eyes. He wondered what odd quirk of fate had brought Jessica Conrad to his house . . . the unwanted wife of the man who had been responsible for Hester's default and the blow to his pride. He was abruptly consumed with the familiar and long-felt anger and loathing . . . and emotions he had believed conquered rose once again within him.

The discovery that Hester was enjoying a tempestuous affair with Conrad had abruptly ended their engagement. He was a very proud man and it was unthinkable that any woman should betray him and be forgiven . . . and he had determined that no other woman should ever get the chance to strike at his pride in like manner. He kept the portrait of Hester in a prominent place as a reminder of past humiliation and his decision to avoid becoming too deeply involved with any woman in the future.

He stared at the canvas now, wondering what had prompted Hester to offer her cottage to Conrad's wife and wondering if she was to blame for the sudden disruption of that marriage or if she had been supplanted long since. He had not seen Hester for months . . . and if Rosa had seen her she had certainly never mentioned the fact to him. He had no wish to see Hester . . . and he completely failed to understand that Jessica Conrad could claim her as a friend in the circumstances. Or had she never known that Hester was her husband's mistress?

Some time later, Gavin made his way to his own room. Passing his sister's room, he paused and knocked lightly on the door. There was no answer. Very softly, he opened the door and looked in . . . the light from the hall illuminated the bed sufficiently for him to see that she slept, her cheek cradled on her hand.

He studied her for a long moment and then he quietly closed the door and, instead of going to his own room, he turned and went back down the stairs. Loosening his tie and shrugging out of his dinner jacket, he went swiftly towards the back of the house, impelled by the powerful urge of the creative artist to take up palette and paints instead of seeking his bed . . .

The sun was high when Jessica woke. She lay in the narrow bed in that delicious lethargy between waking and sleeping. Birds were singing and the bright rays of the sun fell across the bed . . . and for a few moments she questioned nothing. The strange room, the unfamiliar view of tree-tops from the window, the unusual awakening to birdsong were all taken for granted. In Jessica's life there had been many unfamiliar surroundings for she and Ritchie had never known a settled home.

She had slept long and deeply . . . and she thought it must be very late. Ritchie had gone without waking her, she thought drowsily . . . and then she was jerked from her bemused state by abrupt recollection.

Ritchie no longer loved and wanted her . . . Ritchie had betrayed her with other women on numerous occasions and this time he wanted to be free from bonds which had become irksome and boring . . .

Ritchie had finally met a woman who demanded that he end a marriage which stood in the way of her happiness!

Jessica closed her eyes tightly to shut out the image of her husband's handsome, clever face and she drew the blankets over her ears to shut out the echo of that deep, carefully modulated actor's voice telling her the blunt truths that she should have realized for herself long before. She knew that she could never forgive nor forget the devastating blows to her heart and her pride.

She had given herself so completely

to the man she had married, striving to be all that he might want in a woman and a wife, welcoming his desire to mould and shape her to his pattern, wanting only to please and delight him so that he should never want any woman but herself. Giving had come easily and naturally because she loved him and because she had a generous nature and because she felt secure in his love for her.

For six years she had held him close to her heart . . . believing him content, totally unaware of the affairs he enjoyed with other women, she had been completely unprepared for his admission that he had a mistress and meant to marry her as soon as he was free to do so.

That other woman could not love him as she did, Jessica declared fiercely — and one day Ritchie would realize all that he had thrown away. One day he would know how much she really meant to him — but then it would be too late. For although she could not stop loving him she would never trust him again with her happiness and peace of mind.

Their marriage was over and her world lay in pieces at her feet and she felt not the slightest inclination to pick up those pieces and try to make a new life. But she had no choice . . . she must learn to live without him, to endure the bleakness of the future, to find herself again and forget the part she had played for so long. It would not be easy . . . Ritchie had taken a young and impressionable girl of nineteen and moulded her as he wished until, at twenty-five, she could scarcely remember what thoughts, opinions or attitudes had originally been her own. Almost her entire outlook bore his stamp . . . how could she know if a thought or an opinion was her own or an echo of him?

What a fool she had been. What a blind, generous, loving fool . . . terrified of losing something which was probably worthless anyway! Had Ritchie ever really loved her — or had she merely been the ideal lump of clay he could mould into a reflection of his own ego?

She had never known what it meant to be bitter until now . . . now she knew all the slow, destructive corrosion of her faith in human nature and she knew that nothing could ever be the same again, that even her love had been defiled and lessened, that there was no likelihood that she could ever give her affection or her loyalty freely to anyone again. Ritchie had taught her that loving was so much wasted emotion and at last she realized the ugly truth that self was all that really mattered to anyone. It was essential to be self-sufficient, to look after one's own interests . . . it was a mistake to look to others for happiness or security or comfort for they would only fail you when you needed them most!

How innocent, how naive and trusting she had been! But never again she vowed . . . never again! She would not invite heartache and humiliation a second time! The barriers were up . . . !

Throwing back the covers, she went to the window. The garden was well-kept and very pretty in its old-fashioned simplicity, the tall trees were just beginning to burst with new life and the blue sky was strangely cloudless after the grey days that had preceded this one. Jessica realized that it must be spring . . . the season she had always welcomed in the past for its promise and its power to inspire new hopes, new dreams. But she could not welcome it this year for it seemed to promise little for her future and only served to emphasize the bleak desolation that had invaded her heart.

The long, low building that seemed to consist mainly of glass and stood some distance from the house must be Gavin Brice's studio, she thought idly. He was a strange, unpredictable man . . . how many men in similar circumstances would have extended hospitality to an intruder, however innocent?

She fancied that she owed his kindness to her friendship with Hester and she felt a little guilty for she and Hester Carslake had never been on really friendly terms. In fact, Ritchie had never liked the woman and, as always, she had taken her cue from him and avoided any close association with Hester. So it was all the more surprising that it should have been Hester who understood exactly how she felt and been so swift to offer just the right solution to her problem and her need to find a sanctuary.

There was no sign of Gavin Brice when she went down, dressed and carefully made up, her long gleaming hair knotted in a thick coil on the nape of her neck. The open door of the main bedroom had displayed its neatness and a bed that had either been swiftly remade or had not been disturbed at all.

He did not appear to be in the

house. She hesitated briefly and then she stepped out into the garden and made her way to the studio. There was no response to her light knock and she opened the door and looked in, not really expecting him to be there and mildly curious about the surroundings in which he worked. The long drapes were drawn against the sunlight and for a moment her eyes did not adjust to the semi-darkness of the big room. Then she realized that in the midst of a tumble of blankets on a corner divan slept Gavin Brice ... looking remarkably young and oddly vulnerable with his silky fair hair rumpled and touched by the invading sunshine and every line miraculously erased from his handsome face by the soothing embrace of sleep.

Jessica was ridiculously embarrassed. It seemed an intrusion to discover such a man sleeping like an innocent child in the midst of disorder.

She looked curiously about the large, dimly-lit room with its many canvases propped about the walls or on easels or merely stacked in piles.

She decided against waking him. She would write a grateful note and slip away . . . she had imposed on his hospitality quite enough.

Glancing once more at the divan, she found him regarding her with one very blue eye, a smile quirking his lips. "It would be a kindness if you'd make some coffee before you leave," he drawled lazily, just as though he had read her thoughts . . . which indeed he had.

"Oh . . . you're awake," she said, a little foolishly. "I'm sorry — I didn't mean to disturb you."

"You haven't . . . " Extricating an arm from the warm nest of blankets, he reached for cigarettes. "I'm usually up and about by this time," he added, glancing at the wristwatch that he still wore. He held out the case of cigarettes. "Want one?"

Jessica shook her head. "Not now, thanks."

"Is my lighter anywhere about?" he asked. Then, as she peered a little helplessly about the room, he added': "Pull back the drapes, girl — let the blessed sunshine in! It looks a lovely day."

"It is," she told him, surprised to find that she was amused rather than annoyed by his easy familiarity. She drew the heavy curtains back and suddenly the studio was ablaze with light and colour. She discovered the lighter among a tangle of paint-stained cloths . . . and at the same time discovered a rapid and very talented sketch of herself which took her completely by surprise.

Gavin propped himself up on an elbow at her exclamation. "What's that . . . ? Oh, that — there are some more lying about," he said carelessly. "Not very good, though . . . I thought I might do a portrait of you if you're going to be about the neighbourhood for a while. I could trust to memory but I fancy that you'll prove to be a difficult subject. Will you sit — or would it be too much of a bore?"

Jessica sat down on the edge of the divan, her hands full of the sketches which completely held her attention. She would need to be blind or foolish to be unaware that she possessed a certain degree of beauty . . . and indeed she had always been glad of it, knowing that Ritchie demanded beauty in a woman and particularly in his wife. But she had not supposed that it was the kind of beauty that could catch at the imagination as did the girl in these sketches . . . the haunting, wistful, elusive beauty that tugged strangely at the emotions.

"This isn't me . . . " she said wonderingly.

Gavin smiled. "Of course it is — but I warned you that they weren't very good."

She turned to look at him in amazement. "I think they're terrific . . . but much too flattering."

"Perhaps you are much too modest,"

he said lightly. "Did you find that lighter, by the way?"

"Oh . . . yes! Sorry . . . " She tossed it to him, watched absently as he snapped it into flame and drew deeply on the cigarette. Then she rose to her feet. "Do you want some breakfast with your coffee?"

"Can you cook? You aren't dressed for the part," he said, smiling.

Jessica looked down at her very expensive suit with a shrug of dismissal. "I can manage eggs and bacon if you have any."

"There's a plentiful supply of both . . . but you needn't feel obliged to cook for me, you know. I'm not one of your helpless males, thanks to Rosa's training."

"I'd like to do it," she said quietly . . . and turned towards the door.

4

GAVIN did not immediately get up when the door closed behind his beautiful guest. He lay back to finish his cigarette, thoughtfully surveying the covered canvas on which he had worked into the early hours of the morning.

In his mind's eye he could see the preliminary work on the portrait that he had suddenly been inspired to attempt. She was not an easy subject because of some elusive quality in her beauty. But she was a very lovely woman, he thought appreciatively — and she had more than mere beauty.

This morning she looked different . . . and it was not only the elegant suit or the smooth and careful coil of her red-gold hair or the skilful application of cosmetics that her loveliness did not need. She was no longer distraught, of course . . . and he felt that she was already beginning to come to terms with a situation she could not alter. But he fancied that she looked at life with a very jaundiced eye at the moment and she was not to be blamed for bitterness. It was all very well for him to believe that she was better off without a husband like Ritchie Conrad . . . if she loved the man, as one must assume that she did, then it must have hit very hard to learn how unimportant she was to his happiness.

She still looked like a lost, bewildered child, though — and he supposed it was that appealing air of helplessness that was tugging so unexpectedly at his compassion. He was still smarting from that recent affair with Hester but the shadow of pain lurking in those grey eyes, so wide and candid and strangely innocent, could not be brushed aside with complete indifference. He was too tender-hearted, he knew . . . and it was probably asking for trouble but he still wanted to do what he could for Jessica Conrad . . .

She looked very capable and domesticated when he entered the kitchen. He had donned casual slacks and sweater that were in marked contrast to the formal dinner suit of the previous night . . . and he looked taller and even more masculine.

Because Jessica was feeling pleased with herself, discovering that she could cope with the unusual task of preparing a meal for two people, she flashed him a swift, confident smile that took him a little by surprise.

"You look a different woman this morning," he said lightly.

"That would be an ideal solution for many of us, wouldn't it?" she encountered wryly. "To wake a different person . . . new identity, new personality, new hopes and dreams . . . "

"And a whole lot of new problems to cope with, too," he finished drily. "It's taken me all of thirty-four years to come to terms with myself . . . the

60

last thing I'd want is to start all over again in a new skin. Concentrate on cooking and forget the fairy-tales, my child."

It was a timely reminder and Jessica hastily rescued the bacon. She looked at it ruefully and then said on a hopeful note: "Do you like your bacon crisp?"

Gavin laughed. "Just as it comes," he assured her, his eyes twinkling. "You're a better cook than I am, anyway . . . I burn the bacon regularly and always break eggs in the pan."

"You are a comfort," she said gratefully, ladling the hot food on to the plates she had at least thought to warm. "But I suppose you seldom have to look after yourself . . . unless your sister goes away a lot? I've had very little practice at being domesticated. Most of my married life has been spent in hotels and service flats," she added wryly.

"And a great many women would be green with envy to hear you say so," he pointed out, taking his place at the table as she filled the coffee cups.

61

"Yes, I suppose so," she admitted. She was silent for a moment and then she went on: "It's ironic, really . . . there's a homely little body inside me just dying to make a home and raise a family and I chose to marry a man who didn't want a settled home or children."

"Time enough for those things — you'll marry again, I daresay," he said smoothly, carelessly, ignoring the bitterness in her tone. "You're very young, you know."

She shook her head. "Not so young . . . old enough to avoid making the same mistakes again," she returned harshly.

He leaned back in his chair and studied her gravely. "You've been hurt, sure — but that's part of living, Mrs Conrad. You must learn to take the knocks and come up smiling because it's the only way to cope with life. Only a child can afford the luxury of tears because someone is always there to 'kiss it better' . . . we have to make do with pride when we grow too old to cry."

"Oh . . . cold comfort!" she declared wryly.

He nodded. "Perhaps it is but you'll never be lonely," he said sagely.

Jessica looked at him in startled enquiry. "I'm not sure what you mean . . . "

"Hold up your head and laugh and you'll never be without someone to laugh with you," he drawled.

"Weep . . . and I'll weep alone," she finished slowly, thoughtfully.

"Trite — but oh, how true!"

She was silent for a moment. Then her underlip quivering just a fraction, she said quietly: "It's just . . . Just that I don't know what to *do*!"

He understood immediately, she realized. Meeting his blue eyes, she found the warm kindliness in their depths that offered comfort. He understood. She did not need to explain how lost she felt, how strange it was to have to make her own decisions when Ritchie had handled her life for so long.

"Every change is unsettling," he said lightly. "One needs time to think, to decide what to do with the future." He was not usually a man of impulse these days . . . yet it was purely impulse that prompted him to add in the same even tones: "Stay on here for a few days . . . why don't you? Rosa will be home today or tomorrow and I know you will like each other. If you do decide to sit for me you'll be on hand when I want to work . . . and you'll have time to take a look at Hester's cottage and decide if you want to open it up."

Jessica was astonished and oddly pleased by the invitation. But it was so unexpected that she instinctively protested. "You're very kind but I couldn't do that," she said slowly.

"Why not?" he countered, smiling that warm, lazy smile which was so disarmingly attractive.

"You don't really know me," she

said, uncertainly.

Gavin shrugged. "You don't know me," he reminded her lightly. "But we could take each other on trust."

Jessica still hesitated, studying him thoughtfully and with a frankness in her gaze that he found very refreshing. Then suddenly she smiled . . . and for a brief moment the lost child was replaced by an exceptionally beautiful woman with an appeal that was entirely her own.

"Yes . . . " she said slowly, carefully. "We could do that . . . " And, as though to seal the bargain, she held out her hand to him.

Gavin took it and held it for a brief moment — and it was such a small, delicate hand in his strong fingers that he was abruptly and inexplicably moved to tenderness. Their eyes met and held for a moment. He had believed that he could remain immune to any woman after that disastrous experience with Hester and yet he found that Jessica Conrad was tugging insistently at his emotions. He hoped he might not have cause to regret his impulsive invitation . . . he reminded himself that he had resolved to avoid any emotional entanglement in the future.

Jessica was suddenly aware of the genuine warmth in the clasp of his hand and a degree of admiration in his blue eyes that she did not entirely welcome. There might be some comfort to realize that she was attractive to another man but it hinted at complications that she did not want . . . now or ever again. Then she reminded herself that this man had the reputation of a heartless rake and an incorrigible flirt . . . and even if only half the stories were true it did not seem likely that he could be vulnerable. He had said that he was thirty-four . . . a man of that age with all the experience attributed to him did not fall easily in love!

Releasing her, he rose rather abruptly. "I mean to work this morning," he said without ceremony. "I want to get on with your portrait. But I won't need you at the moment, Mrs Conrad. I have the sketches and there's a lot of preliminary work to be done. Please make yourself at home — and if you do want me you'll know where to find me!"

He left her, striding swiftly out of the house and heading for the studio without another word or a backward glance. Jessica was taken aback and just a little dismayed by the sudden desertion. She realized that one must make allowances for the artistic temperament but his abrupt departure had been almost ill-mannered!

Then she laughed at herself . . . as if it mattered! It was almost a relief to realize that his unconventional manners released her from any formal obligation and that he meant her to feel quite free to come and go just as she pleased, to do exactly as she wished. It was just what she wanted — and she had the odd, fleeting suspicion that Gavin Brice knew what she needed and intended that she should find it at Redvers House . . .

She enjoyed her morning. It was a rare luxury to be entirely alone, to follow her own inclinations, to feel so incredibly and deliciously free. Obviously the novelty would eventually wear off and she would be lonely and bored and aware of the emptiness in her days but for the moment she could luxuriate in her freedom.

She pottered about the house, delighting in the game of keeping house, almost wishing there was more to do than make a bed, tidy a kitchen and flick a duster about the furniture, perfectly aware that it would not have been so delightful if it was necessity rather than choice.

She wandered in the garden, plucking the occasional weed and rather pleased with herself that she could recognize them, admiring the informality and the prettiness of a garden which appeared to have 'happened' rather than been planned . . . She started to walk down the lane in the apparent direction of Brook Cottage, curious to compare it with Redvers House, but swiftly changed her mind as her high heels sank into the muddy channels. She must buy herself some brogues if she meant to stay long in this part of the world, she told herself, ruefully regarding her shoes . . . and it was some moments before it occurred to her that she felt so much at home that she might have lived in Redvers House all her life.

Her thoughts were not long away from Ritchie, of course . . . again and again she tortured herself with that last painful encounter with the man she loved so desperately. But with each mental review of all that had passed between them it became increasingly more clear that their marriage was irrevocably at an end and that she must think of making a new life for herself. Even if Ritchie regretted parting with her and wanted her back she knew it was impossible to live with him again . . . how could any woman return to a man who had told her cruelly and with obvious truth that she bored him to death!

She wondered what Ritchie's reactions were to her sudden disappearance . . . if he knew or even cared that she had run away from the intolerable publicity? Perhaps he simply accepted that she had gone to stay with friends — the curt message that she had left for anyone who sought to know her whereabouts.

She had found a friend, certainly, she thought with a sudden rush of gratitude for a stranger who had shown such kindness and understanding. There was a much-needed reassurance and comfort in his casual acceptance of her presence. He was obviously an unconventional man . . . but she knew she could trust him. Perhaps it was his size, she thought with a faint smile . . . there was something inevitably reassuring about those broad shoulders and that massive chest and the strong, handsome face. He looked the kind of man that anyone would instinctively turn to in trouble . . . and for all his size and obvious strength he possessed an innate tenderness and a gentle touch and a smile that tugged ridiculously at one's heart. He was a friend, she thought warmly . . . the kind of man one instinctively regarded as a friend and confidant.

She wondered how his sister would react to her presence when she eventually returned to her home. It might be Gavin Brice's house and his right to invite whom he wished to stay — but a sister might be possessive, resentful of strangers and strongly disapproving of a young woman who had ignored all the conventions to stay unchaperoned with her brother.

She visualized Rosa Brice as a sour, tight-lipped spinster who had devoted her life to looking after her brother and protecting him from the unscrupulous women who might involve him in any scandal. Well, she might be an excellent housekeeper but she could not protect him from scandal if the press ever discovered that the wife of Ritchie

Conrad had spent the night beneath his roof. No one would ever believe that they were not lovers, she thought wryly. No one would ever believe that a man with his reputation had slept in his studio at the far end of the garden while she slept in the house!

She found it difficult to reconcile the man she knew and liked with the artist who was described as an unscrupulous rake. But she reminded herself that she scarcely knew him and she had already felt the attraction of the man and it was obvious that a womanizer must possess a great deal of charm — as he undoubtedly did. He was very much a man . . . she could not suppose that he lived a celibate life. He was a very handsome man and she found it easy to believe that many women had fallen victim to his charm and good looks.

She was protected by her feeling for Ritchie. But if she were young and single and free to love it might be incredibly easy to love a man like Gavin Brice.

The sun climbed higher and Jessica began to wonder about lunch. Did the artist ignore his inner man when he was working . . . or was he expecting her to call him in for a meal very soon? She supposed she ought to find out. She went down the garden to the studio and knocked a little hesitantly on the open door. He was working at an easel, painting with swift, sure strokes. He glanced round and sent her a warm but somewhat preoccupied smile.

"I'm disturbing your . . . " she said quickly.

"No — I don't find that people are a distraction," he assured her lightly. "I've been waiting for you, anyway . . . what have you been doing with yourself all morning?"

"Relaxing," she told him with a little laugh.

"Excellent! I'm a rotten host, I'm afraid . . . I usually leave my guests to amuse themselves in their own way."

"Liberty Hall, in fact," she suggested, smiling. She looked around the large and very light studio, interested in the many canvases. She had supposed that he only concentrated on portraits but it seemed that he dabbled in all kinds of subjects and a variety of mediums and she could not help admiring the skill and the delicacy of his work.

"Well . . . ?" he prompted after a few moments.

She turned, smiling. "I'm not qualified to pass opinions . . . I just know what I like. Some of your paintings are beautiful . . . some are baffling. But even without the public acclaim you've achieved I'd know you are a great artist," she finished simply.

"I paint to please myself . . . if it also pleases others, well and good. But I should still paint what I like the way I like even if the world shuddered," he said bluntly. "Come here, will you . . . I want to look at you," he added, rather brusquely.

She was a little startled but she went to him. He set aside his palette and turned to her, taking her chin in his strong fingers and moving her face so that the bright sunlight fell across it. They were very close and she was suddenly very much aware of the magnetism in this man and her pulse quickened in faint apprehension. But his touch was entirely impersonal and there was nothing but pure concentration in his blue eyes. She stood very still while he traced the curve of her cheek with his fingers, his eyes intent on her face . . . and she had the strangest impression that he saw through those gentle fingers rather than his eyes. He held her firmly by the shoulder . . . she could not move away from him even if she wished and such was the compelling personality of — the man that she did not wish to break the spell of his concentration.

Gavin regarded her as nothing more than the object of his artistic instincts in that moment . . . and then, satisfied, suddenly elated, he became abruptly aware of her as a woman — a breathing, living, very feminine person whose uplifted face was very near to his own. Sudden, urgent desire swept through him, startling in its intensity . . . his hand tightened on her slender shoulder and the warm glow in his blue eyes compelled her compliance as he bent his handsome head to kiss her . . .

"Hullo there! Gavin! I'm home . . ."

The cheerful cry broke through the magic of the moment just as their lips were about to touch. Jessica found herself abruptly released as he said almost roughly: "My sister . . ."

Strangely shaken by her unexpected response to his physical magnetism and deeply dismayed to realize that he was indeed the womanizer he was reputed to be, Jessica drew away from him just as his sister appeared in the doorway . . . young, pretty and so utterly unlike the sour, tight-lipped spinster she had visualized that Jessica stared in obvious surprise . . .

5

ROSA BRICE was small and slender, petite and very pretty, her pale blonde hair cut short to frame the small face and the very blue eyes emphasized by the delicacy of pink and white colouring. Jessica was reminded of the porcelain miniatures she had loved to collect until Ritchie had sneered at her liking for such trivia.

She was not at all embarrassed although she must be aware that she had interrupted a tense moment. She threw her brother a laughing glance and declared lightly: "To think I rushed home because I thought you might be lonely!"

Gavin grinned. "It took you almost a fortnight to remember that you have a home," he teased her warmly.

"It was a long weekend, wasn't it?"

she agreed, her eyes dancing with laughter. "Brent came over from New York unexpectedly and I couldn't rush away."

"Nor did you want to," he said drily but his smile held warm understanding. "Welcome home, anyway . . . ! I don't know if you already know each other, by the way," he said, drawing Jessica to his sister's notice with a glance. "My sister, Rosa . . . Jessica Conrad."

Rosa said lightly: "We haven't actually met officially . . . but we were at the same party once, if you remember? It was rather a chaotic affair — Eunice Sheldon's party at her house in Hampstead last spring."

Jessica was just a little disconcerted . . . and also relieved that Gavin Brice had not allowed her to conceal her identity. It would have been embarrassing, to say the least, to be exposed by his sister. "I remember the party," she said slowly — and she was also remembering Ritchie had been noticeably attentive to a well-known actress at that particular party. "I don't think anyone was actually introduced to anyone else but by the time the party ended we were all bosom friends," she added lightly.

Rosa laughed. "Yes, that's true . . . it was that kind of a party." She moved forward to study the canvas on her brother's easel. "You're sitting for Gavin, I see . . . oh, early stages yet! But it promises to be good," she assured her brother, smiling up at him with the confident air of an expert.

"Thank you," he said drily. "You are reassuring. But it needs a great deal of work yet. I'm hoping to persuade Mrs Conrad to stay until the portrait is finished . . . she has promised me a few days but I'm afraid it will take longer than that."

"Oh, but you must stay!" Rosa said swiftly, warmly, turning to Jessica. "If it's at all possible, anyway Gavin will work to all hours — he always does when he's really interested in a subject. I shall be glad of your company when he doesn't need you to sit for him."

Jessica smiled involuntarily at the other girl's eagerness. "We'll see," she temporized.

"Oh, good!" Rosa exclaimed as though it was quite settled. "Has anyone eaten yet, by the way? I didn't stop on the road for lunch and I'm absolutely famished."

Gavin glanced at his wristwatch. "We haven't had lunch . . . I didn't realize it was so late, actually."

"I was about to ask you if you wanted some food," Jessica explained hastily.

"We'll organize something . . . cold cuts and salad, perhaps. Quick and virtually effortless. If you are finished with Mrs Conrad for the time being she might like to help me, Gavin?"

"I wish you would call me Jessica," she interposed impulsively, partly because she desired the friendship that brother and sister seemed to offer so generously and partly because she disliked the continual reminder of something she needed so much to forget. "Both of you . . . " she added with a glance at the artist that almost reproached him for the formality he seemed to insist upon even though they had rapidly reached a degree of intimacy that was a little alarming.

But there was nothing alarming in the immediate understanding that leaped between herself and Rosa Brice. Jessica felt that they must have known each other for years and she found the warm, easy, friendly acceptance that Rosa offered both comforting and comfortable. She sensed that her liking for Rosa was readily reciprocated and as they were much of an age it was natural that they should have a great deal in common.

It would be foolish to doubt that Rosa knew she was Ritchie Conrad's wife and she must surely know that their marriage had broken up in a blaze of publicity. But she seemed entirely without curiosity and there was nothing in her manner that compelled any explanation on Jessica's part. Later, thought Jessica, she would tell Rosa of the foolish mistake that had brought her to Redvers House and they would laugh over it but for the moment it seemed wholly unimportant.

Rosa was curious, very naturally . . . but much too sensitive to ask tactless or unwelcome questions. She realized that, whatever the circumstances of the Conrad separation, Jessica had suffered and was still suffering because of it . . . and being as tenderhearted as her brother she would not dream of probing wounds.

It was really none of her business how she came to be at Redvers House . . . or how well she really knew Gavin. It did cross her mind to wonder if Gavin had anything to do with the break-up of the Conrad's domestic bliss . . . he was devastatingly attractive, after all, and inclined to be a little ruthless and unscrupulous if he wanted anything badly enough. She hated to think that her brother might have revenged the loss of Hester to Ritchie Conrad in a particularly unpleasant manner . . . but she could not really be blamed for thinking it possible. He had been deeply hurt by Hester's affair with the film star, she knew . . . and it spoke volumes that of all the women who had played some part in his life there had only been one woman whom he had wanted to marry — and that was Hester Carslake. It was obvious that he had been very much in love with her . . . his refusal to discuss his broken engagement or even to talk about Hester proved that her disloyalty had really hit him hard.

Rosa did not want to believe that Gavin had repaid Ritchie Conrad in kind by seducing his wife . . . but it was odd that less than six months later the Conrad marriage was breaking up and Jessica Conrad was staying at Redvers House. She was not particularly anxious about the scandal which might involve her brother but she was anxious that Gavin should not be hurt a second time. She wished that he had steered clear of the woman who was known to be hopelessly, even pathetically, in love with a virtually indifferent husband.

And she said as much to her brother at the first opportunity, feeling impelled to warn him but fully expecting an unmistakable rebuff.

But Gavin did not rebuff her . . . not exactly. He was simply evasive. He listened with faint amusement dawning in his eyes as he realized how busy her lively imagination had been.

"So you think I am 'involved', do you?" he drawled, stretching his long legs and settling deeper in his chair.

"I know in my bones that you are," she returned bluntly.

He raised an eyebrow. "Your bones aren't particularly reliable," he reminded her lightly. "Only last year they assured you that I meant to marry Hester . . . but that didn't happen, did it?"

"You did mean to marry Hester . . . and I knew it long before you admitted as much to me," she said stubbornly. "I don't want to rub salt into old wounds, Gavin . . . but you did blame Ritchie Conrad for interfering with your plans. Hester would have married you by now if she hadn't become entangled with him . . . and I know how you felt about the man. Oh, Gavin — I don't want you mixed up in the mess of the Conrad marriage!"

"But I'm not," he assured her carelessly. "And not likely to be, believe me. The mess is none of my making."

She looked at him doubtfully. "Conrad will drag you into it if he can," she said sharply. "It's no secret that he wants to get rid of his wife and he will seize on the least excuse to divorce her, you know. He'd cite you on the flimsiest of evidence . . . and her presence here at this particular time isn't exactly flimsy evidence, is it? You'd have the devil's own job to convince the world of your innocence if it leaked out that she's staying here!"

"Then I should have the comfort of a clear conscience," he drawled, smiling. "She did not come here by my invitation, Rosa."

She studied her fingernails intently. He would not lie to her, she knew . . . but she did think he must be understating the case. He might not have known that Jessica Conrad would run to him when she was faced with a crisis in her marriage but he had certainly not turned her away, she thought wryly.

"I suppose you know that she's crazy about Conrad," she said tautly. "Everyone knows that she adores him! You'll only get hurt again, Gavin . . ."

He raised an eyebrow. "Your imagination is running away with you, Rosa," he said lightly. "My interest in Mrs Conrad is merely artistic . . . I am satisfying my desire to paint her beautiful face and providing her with an excellent excuse to remain out of town until interest in her marital affairs has died down."

Rosa was far from satisfied but

Jessica's arrival with the coffee forced her to drop the subject for the moment.

Brother and sister had always been very close. Far from being jealous of the new baby after ten years of being the only and much-loved child, Gavin had adored his tiny sister and instantly instituted himself her protector from all ills. Losing the father she idolized when she was still very young, Rosa had instinctively turned to Gavin to fill the role and he had done so with wisdom and tenderness, helping her through the difficult years of their mother's remarriage and subsequent loss of interest in her children.

Gavin had also been by her side to comfort and sustain Rosa when the man she planned to marry was killed only three days before their wedding . . . and it had been his suggestion that she should keep house for him. It had also been his suggestion that she should utilize her own artistic gifts in some way and Rosa had discovered with his encouragement that she had a flair for illustrating children's books.

Four years had passed since Barry's death . . . she remembered him with tenderness but she was ready to love again and Brent Wakefield was becoming important to her. But there was plenty of time — and she felt that she owed too much to Gavin to leave him abruptly in the lurch. She knew how much he relied on her, all unconsciously . . . and she knew how much he would hate looking after himself or employing someone to keep house for him. Living together had proved an ideal arrangement for the brother and sister for no one could expect a man like Gavin to bother his head with domestic affairs and Rosa had found that she possessed a flair for housekeeping and enjoyed combining mundane matters with her artistic talents.

Gavin would wish her happy and mean it and assure her that he was capable of managing without her for he was the kindest man in the world. But she could not stifle her conscience for she suspected that he had only bought Redvers House in the first instance to provide her with security and a new interest at a time when she needed such things quite desperately.

She had supposed that the problem would solve itself when he married Hester . . . but his plans had come to an abrupt and painful end. Knowing him to be very proud and much more sensitive than he would admit to the world, Rosa often wondered if he would find it possible to love again sufficiently to think of marriage. He had scarcely looked at a woman since breaking with Hester and Rosa would have been delighted if she had found him on the verge of making love to any other woman but Jessica Conrad.

She had recognized her instantly . . . and felt an instinctive dismay which she hoped that she had successfully concealed. For while she had not been at all surprised to learn from the press that the Conrads had decided to part, it had been a shock to find the celebrity's wife not only at Redvers House but virtually in her brother's arms!

She had known an immediate rapport with Jessica Conrad at that first, brief meeting and the tentative overtures of friendship exchanged on that occasion might have led to a warmer association if they had moved in the same circles. Meeting her again, Rosa could not help liking her. In different circumstances, she would have welcomed her to Redvers House and encouraged Gavin's obvious interest — even hoped that Jessica could persuade him to forget Hester. As it was, she could only hope that she had put the wrong construction on appearances, that Gavin and Jessica were merely friends, that Gavin was more interested in portraying the woman than making love to her and that he might not make the disastrous mistake of falling for a woman who would probably run straight back to her husband at the merest lift of his finger . . .

Rousing herself, Rosa announced that she would clear away and wash the dishes. Jessica was sent into the sunny garden, bidden to 'sit and watch the flowers grow'.

Smiling, she did as she was told and sank into the deckchair that Gavin brought for her, thanking him a little shyly. There had been some constraint between them during the meal for she had felt oddly reluctant to meet his eyes and he had seldom addressed a remark directly to her. Rosa's light chatter had successfully covered the fact that they were slightly ill at ease with each other . . . momentarily alone, it was abruptly obvious.

Gavin looked down at her, a faint frown in his eyes. "You mean to stay, I hope?" he asked, a trifle brusquely. "You are very welcome, you know."

Her mouth twisted a little wryly. "You are both so kind . . . " She broke off, hesitating.

91

"Too kind?" he demanded swiftly, acutely. "Are we making it difficult for you to insist on your own preference? You must feel free to stay or go, you know — just as you please." Suddenly he smiled. "This is Liberty Hall, remember!"

That warm, attractive smile tugged unexpectedly at her emotions. "Thank you . . . I should like to stay," she said simply.

Briefly he rested a hand on her shoulder. He was pleased by the decision. He knew instinctively that there was something in these surroundings that she needed . . . the stillness of sanctuary that it provided, perhaps; the quiet waters which took no heed of the turbulent currents behind and before. He loved his home for that very quality, so essential to a man of his temperament . . . even Hester had not managed to destroy its serenity with her insidious evil.

He left Jessica, making his way towards the studio, and she watched him go with mixed feelings. He was a sensitive, perceptive man, she thought — but he had mistaken the cause of her hesitation. For she did not feel that the Brices were placing her under any obligation . . . indeed, she very simply felt that she had come home. It was an odd unshakeable conviction that of all the places in the world this was where she belonged just now — and the Brices seemed to have been part of her life for as long as she could remember.

She had told Gavin Brice that she would stay yet deep down she felt it might not have been a wise decision. For all its calm and beauty, Redvers House held a certain danger. Gavin Brice had very nearly kissed her — and she had very nearly welcomed the touch of his lips, all other considerations swept aside by the magnetism of the man and the magic of the moment.

She loved Ritchie, would always love him — and yet she had found it possible to know the leaping urgency of desire for another man's embrace. She had been shocked — and a little frightened. It had been an alarming experience for a woman who had welcomed her husband's lovemaking only for the delight he found in her arms, never quite understanding the intoxication of desire for him. Her love had never been rooted in physical attraction — and she had naively and foolishly supposed it superior to most loving for that reason. Still immature in some ways, she had thought only of giving — and never realized that she might be denying Ritchie the privilege of giving in his turn or that he might have sought other women because he disliked the knowledge that his wife bestowed her favours rather than shared the delights and pleasures of passion.

Jessica had supposed herself to be a frigid woman by nature, something that no one could help nor alter. It had been a terrific jolt to her complacency to discover that the mere touch of a man's hand could evoke the swift flood of desire. She wanted Gavin Brice as she had never wanted the husband she loved . . . and while she might despise her weakness and determine to fight it with all her might, she had awoken to a new understanding and a new maturity.

6

RITCHIE CONRAD was an undeniably handsome man. Tall, dark-haired, dark-eyed, he possessed the kind of romantic good looks that most women found irresistible and he gave an impression of masculine toughness that most women found convincing. He also had a very bewitching smile.

But as he stepped from the huge airliner to be greeted by a barrage of flashing cameras and shrewd pressmen, his smile was merely automatic and did not touch the eyes that held more than a hint of angry impatience.

This kind of publicity could do him no good whatsoever, he thought grimly, furious with Jessica for behaving so hysterically. He had put more faith in her discretion and in her own desire to avoid public comment — and, perhaps, in her usually reliable regard for his wishes. He had not expected his desire to be free to make headlines at this stage; indeed, he had hoped to escape with a mere half-inch mention on an inside page when the divorce eventually went through.

He ran the gauntlet of reporters, dealing with the rapid questions and penetrating comment with practised skill and finally felt that he had managed to convey the impression that while his marital affairs were a little upset at the moment it might well turn out to be a storm in a teacup.

Relaxing in his chauffeur-driven car as it took him back to town, he wished that might be the end of it but he knew the inescapable probing into one's private affairs was the price one had to pay for the kind of fame that he had worked so hard to attain.

He had hinted at an early reconciliation . . . and he smiled to himself a little grimly. For in fact he had not the least intention of going on with a marriage that had become a thorn in his flesh.

Ritchie Conrad had fallen heavily in love — and, he believed, really in love for the first time in his life. There had been plenty of women — too many women — but he had never felt so deeply and passionately involved with any woman until now and his need for her had swiftly become an obsession.

He knew very well that she skilfully fanned the flame of passion for her while keeping him just at arms' length and he also knew that she had marriage in mind and that nothing less would satisfy her. He wanted marriage, too. There had never been anyone like his beautiful, ardent, exciting Hester with all the promise of an incredible ecstasy only to be found in her arms . . . but not until he had freed himself from the clinging arms of his wife.

During the past few months he had tried again and again to tell Jessica that he wanted a divorce. He had known it would not be easy: he had not realized that it would be quite so difficult. For Jessica's entire world revolved about him. But at last the passionate need for Hester which never ceased to torment him had driven him beyond the sticking point — and he had been thankful that Jessica had been too stunned to protest. Of course, there had been very little time for her to say or do anything, he recalled wryly. For he had deliberately waited until they were together at the airport and he had but a few moments before boarding his plane for Cyprus. He had explained the circumstances to her in a few, well-chosen, succinct words . . . and she had stared at him in shocked disbelief, her eyes darkening and her face whitening as those words registered their impact. With a hasty assurance that they would discuss the matter at greater length when he got back, Ritchie had thankfully dashed for the barrier and his waiting plane.

He had glanced back briefly . . . and her small, utterly bewildered and wholly stricken figure had caused him a great deal of discomfort during the flight. He had been deliberately cruel in his choice of words, knowing that she would seize on any vagueness or ambiguity to assure herself that he was not in earnest, that it was merely a temporary disillusion with their marriage that he felt and that he could not really desire the finality of a divorce. It would have been much more cruel to allow her to nurture false hopes only to discover later that he was wholly determined on his freedom.

Once in Cyprus and plunged into his work on the new film, he had forgotten that look of anguish in his wife's eyes and found himself looking forward eagerly to a glorious future with Hester. But those idyllic dreams were soon marred by the realization that Jessica had immediately blurted out her grievances to the Press and incurred a great deal of unwelcome publicity for them both.

His reputation as an actor need not suffer because his private life was not impeccable, he knew. But fans were fickle and one never knew quite how they would react to certain items of publicity. He had always known that the majority of his fans approved of his marriage to someone with whom they could identify for there was nothing glamorous or sophisticated about Jessica. She was lovely to look at but there was a quiet simplicity about her and a gentle modesty which never encroached on his claim to attention. It was very likely that he would be much criticized and condemned for wanting to be free of her for the sake of another woman.

He had not mentioned Hester's name when he talked of divorce to Jessica and fortunately there was nothing to link them in any way. Hester had insisted from the beginning that no one should suspect that they were any more than casual acquaintances and she was quite determined not to be cited in the courts by a jealous wife. He must obtain his freedom but not via her reputation!

He reached his town flat to discover

that Jessica had left London without leaving an address where she might be found. Mentally he shrugged his shoulders . . . he had no particular desire to find her just yet. It had probably been a sensible move on her part to put herself beyond the reach of the Press — much more sensible than the hysterical outpourings which had done so much damage, he thought with renewed anger.

He telephoned Hester. They talked for a long time, finally agreeing that it would not be wise to meet until the first heat of publicity had cooled down a little. He did not mention his wife by name and Hester said nothing about her part in Jessica's sudden flight from town.

As his anger cooled and the days passed without any word from Jessica, Ritchie began to feel some degree of anxiety. To some extent, he felt responsible for the woman he had married even though he no longer cared for her or wished to live with her. He could not wholly ignore the fact that for six years Jessica had been totally dependent on him for everything — most of all, for her happiness and peace of mind. He was not too happy about her continued absence from town and the fact that she neither telephoned nor wrote to let him know her whereabouts. He began to make discreet enquiries but no one seemed to have any idea where Jessica could be — and it did not occur to him that Hester would know for she and Jessica had never been on close terms of friendship, thanks to his intervention. Jessica was quick to make friends and she would have encouraged Hester to become one of her intimate circle but it had not suited Ritchie to visualize his wife and his would be mistress indulging in cosy girl-talk over the teacups.

Hester pretended complete ignorance of Jessica's whereabouts, supposing her to be safely installed at the cottage in Bednoken and licking her wounds in privacy. She had not given a thought to the condition of the cottage . . . having dismissed it from her mind for months it had simply not occurred to her that the winter damp and cold might have caused some deterioration in the place. She had almost forgotten that she owned a country cottage until Jessica's predicament urged her to remember the fact. It had suited her very well to pack Ritchie Conrad's wife off to the country for the time being — and it had also suited her to allow Jessica to swear her to secrecy.

She had seen little signs of it but she supposed that Ritchie had a conscience like everyone else . . . and she did not want him taking up with Jessica again in a fit of remorse. It had taken her long enough to persuade him to shake her off!

She was a little surprised by his sudden concern to know where his wife had gone but did not suppose for a moment that he wanted Jessica back . . . it was merely that his conscience was pricking him, she decided comfortably . . .

Another day passed — and Ritchie's anxiety deepened. If Jessica was not with friends or the aunt who was her only relative — and he had checked very carefully — then he could not imagine where she might be or with whom. He told himself that it was foolish to worry about her . . . she was a grown woman and well able to take care of herself. But he was worried and he would very much like to know that she was safe and well.

She had taken her car and some of her clothes and her cheque book had gone from the bureau although she had left her passport behind . . . it did not seem likely that there could be any sinister explanation of her disappearance. And yet he began to be afraid . . . and the fear was growing rapidly. For only he knew just how deeply involved Jessica had always been with him . . . that he was the pivot about which her life revolved, that he was the sun, moon and stars to the girl he had married.

Those people who hinted that she might be with another man simply did not know what they were talking about, he thought grimly. Other men just did not exist for Jessica. She had adored him from the first moment of meeting him and nothing had ever dimmed his god-like image in her eyes. It had been damned uncomfortable to live with, he remembered with a hint of the familiar irritation . . . and virtually impossible to live up to! Early on in their marriage he had ceased to try!

He had married her because she so obviously adored him and never questioned anything he did or said. He had foolishly imagined that a man could not want more in a wife . . . she had been young, warm-hearted, enchantingly lovely, wholly innocent and very sweet. The very contrast to the women who swarmed about him with blatant promise in their too-experienced eyes had been the snare he had been unable to avoid. But he might not have meant marriage if he had not stupidly dangled that carrot before her in a moment of urgent desire and then found it impossible to disappoint and disillusion the vulnerable, radiant child that she had been in those days.

It had been a mistake, of course. Within a very short time he had found himself entangled in the sticky strands of her overwhelming love for him ... and realized that she continually made demands on him by demanding nothing from him. He had never been able to decide if she was incredibly naive or devilishly clever. She was so loving, so eager to please, so undemanding — and so damnably sensitive to the merest irritation in his tone and so absurdly insensitive to his boredom with her youth and innocence. He had once likened her to a blindly adoring puppy who refuses to understand a kick and insists on coming back for more — an attitude that invited and encouraged a latent cruelty in his nature, unfortunately.

He had soon realized that she did not feel the usual kind of love that a woman knows for a man. Physically they were totally incompatible . . . she simply could not understand or respond to the desire that she swiftly evoked in him. He had discovered that his wife was frigid and knowing that he would never have married her if he had discovered that fact earlier he never quite forgave her for trapping him into so unsatisfactory a marriage.

It had been a difficult situation. He had been fond of her in his own way, admiring the sweet and loving generosity of her nature even while he vaguely despised her for bestowing it on a man who did not merit so much love and loyalty. As a cynic, he had always been contemptuous of her romantic faith in the power of love. Yet he had depended on her love and loyalty even while he professed to be stifled by it and frequently betrayed it without compunction.

She needed the security and the devotion that he had been incapable of providing. She should have married anyone but a man like himself, settled down to quiet domesticity and raised a couple of well-behaved children. Marriage had bored him: he wanted the stimulus of travel, fresh faces, new experiences and could not settle in any one place for long; he had never felt any desire for children, feeling that they would be very much out of place in his life . . . and perhaps aware that Jessica's devotion would no longer be centred on him and loth to lose any part of it even while it irked him so much. In truth, he simply never had the time to give to a wife who demanded not only his time but an interest and an affection of which he was simply not capable and all this without ever appearing to demand anything of him!

Inevitably there had been other women . . . inevitably there had been Hester who knew, understood and shared his outlook on life. Hester did make demands on him and insisted that he fulfil them and then met him halfway . . . but that was loving as he understood it. The kind of adoration that he obviously inspired in Jessica was not the kind of loving that he wanted . . . and he hoped that she would eventually wake to the truth that it was no kind of loving between a man and a woman.

There was satisfaction in loving Hester . . . she was honest and she played fair, knowing the rules of the game and abiding by them. There had been very little satisfaction in his marriage to a child like Jessica. Oh, she had matured, of course . . . compelled to do so because he had soon tired of a young wife who expected so much of him and he had gone his own way and left her to make what she could of the situation. She had chosen to tag along, doing her best to keep up with him, closing her eyes to the many flaws in their marriage, trying so hard to be the kind of wife that she believed he wanted . . . and binding him around with silken cords until he had longed for escape at any cost even though he found it almost impossible to destroy her by demanding his freedom.

Then he had met and loved Hester and finally known that he must be free to marry her — and now he was beginning to be afraid that he had destroyed the wife who loved him not wisely but too well . . .

"Darling, do stop pacing up and down like a caged tiger," Hester said silkily. Curled in a deep armchair, her beautiful eyes regarded him steadily through a faint haze of cigarette smoke. It was their first meeting since he had returned from Cyprus . . . and it was not going at all according to plan, she thought impatiently.

Ritchie paused in his tracks. "Sorry . . . I know it's absurd," he admitted ruefully. "But I can't help wondering where the devil she can be, you know. It's more than a week since she left town without a word to anyone as far as I can discover."

Hester shrugged. She was very, very bored with the subject of his wife. "I expect she's enjoying her freedom and hasn't given you a thought in days," she said carelessly.

"I wish I could believe it!" he exclaimed.

"And I wish I could say the same for you," she returned drily.

The sarcasm escaped him. Frowning, he poured himself a drink . . . the third within ten minutes. "It isn't like Jessica not to let me know where she is," he said quietly, more to himself than to Hester. "She'll expect me to be worried about her, you see."

"And you are, aren't you?" she said sweetly . . . and sudden, icy anger leaped to her green eyes.

He was oblivious to her anger as he had been to her sarcasm. "To some extent, naturally." He sipped his drink thoughtfully. "You don't understand darling. Jessica is a very sensitive girl, highly-strung, impulsive, emotionally-guided . . . she might have done something very foolish . . . " He broke off as she swung her long legs to the floor and stood up, gathering her lovely furs about her slim shoulders in a gesture of finality. "You aren't going!" he exclaimed swiftly, dismayed.

"I have an appointment," she said coolly. "And I refuse to be bored any longer . . . I came to be entertained and you are very dull company. If you are so concerned about Jessica then it astonishes me that you ever brought yourself to mention the subject of divorce."

He reached for her swiftly, drew her inexorably towards him . . . but although she stood in the circle of his arms her body was stiff and unyielding and her eyes were hard and cold. Sudden fear leaped in him . . . the fear of losing her, after all. His arms tightened about her urgently. "I am dull company . . . I don't know how you ever came to fall in love with me," he said lightly, smiling, holding her gaze intently with his own, placing every reliance on the charm that so many women had found irresistible.

For a moment longer, she resisted him. Then she laughed softly and relaxed against him. "I hate you, Ritchie Conrad," she murmured against his lips. "We have so little time and you waste it talking of another woman . . . "

"Then we must make the most of the time that's left," he said softly . . . and claimed her willing lips with an urgency that left her breathless.

7

IT was just a year since Hester had first decided to marry Ritchie Conrad. The fact that he already had a wife had not appeared to her as any bar to her happiness for she invariably managed to get what she wanted from life with little difficulty.

The only child of a wealthy and influential politician, she had discovered at an early age that she could get anything she wanted merely by frowning on those who had already learned to depend on her smiles. She had the combined gifts of looks and charm and she had always been able to win liking and admiration without trying for it . . . and thus whenever something came along that she wanted she simply withdrew the favour of her friendship and the affection from the one person who could secure it for her and instantly he or she would hasten to win back a place in her affections by doing or getting what she wanted.

It was a ploy that worked well for Hester while it would have failed miserably for many others. And she never doubted that it would work where Ritchie Conrad was concerned.

Confidence was vital to the plans of a woman like Hester . . . and because she was so confident of her ability to attract and acquire any man she chose, it had been no surprise that Ritchie sought her out within days of their first encounter and was soon head over heels in passionate love. The surprise came later when she unexpectedly realized that she loved him almost as passionately . . . until then she had not equated her determination to marry him with any deep emotional involvement on her part. She had merely decided to become Mrs Ritchie Conrad with all the attendant wealth and glamour and social standing.

In love, she still managed to keep her

head and their relationship never quite passed the point of no return despite the urgency of their mutual desire. She handled him skilfully and she was prepared to be patient, to wait until the thought of marrying her entered his head without any prompting on her part. Eventually it did. He said very little but she knew that marriage was in his mind and everything was going just as she had planned, moving inexorably towards that golden future she intended that they should share. And then Ritchie had woken to the full realization of an unpleasant fact . . . that in order to be free to marry her he must hurt and humiliate the wife who adored him. While claiming to be deeply in love with her, he had nevertheless felt wholly unable to ask Jessica for a divorce . . . and so Hester had broken with him with a ruthlessness he had not expected and which had appalled him.

She had been unhappy but she had not allowed Ritchie to know it. She had been thoroughly in despair when the announcement of her engagement to Gavin Brice, some weeks later, had brought only a brief congratulatory note from Ritchie. She had been baffled. Knowing how miserable she was and convinced that his life was equally bleak without her, she could not understand that he showed no sign of weakening. They only had to meet, as they inevitably did, and she knew by the look in his eyes that his feelings for her were unchanged. But he was bound more tightly than she had realized by the bonds of his marriage.

For the first time in her life, it had been Hester who weakened . . . Hester who found that she could not go on loving from a distance, could not be comforted by anyone else, could not face a future that did not allow her to bask in Ritchie's smiles, to know the strength of his arms about her and to feel the security of being loved by the man she loved. She abruptly ended the engagement which had not proved to be as useful as she had anticipated and humbled her pride to regain her former position in Ritchie's life.

She still refused to become his mistress. Without consciously admitting it to herself she knew that his desire for her was her greatest hold over him and perhaps her only path to the goal she had not entirely ceased to expect. The months slipped by and just when she had begun to believe that he was resigned to the unsatisfactory state of affairs he had suddenly declared his determination to obtain his freedom.

She had not allowed herself to believe it. Therefore she had been as surprised as everyone else when the story of the Conrad separation broke in the newspapers. Elated, triumphant, determined that he should have no opportunity or encouragement to retract, she had seized on the chance to assist his wife to leave town before he returned to England.

It had not occurred to her that Ritchie would be genuinely anxious about Jessica's sudden departure for an unknown destination. Hester was sick with fear beneath that calm, sophisticated self-assurance. Had she underestimated Jessica's hold over the man to whom she had been married for six years? Was it possible that Ritchie's feeling for his wife went deeper than the passion *she* had evoked, after all? Did he love his wife . . . perhaps without being consciously aware of all that she meant to him?

Hester wondered if she had made another mistake. It had been a mistake to break with Ritchie months before, to engage herself cold-bloodedly to another man in the belief that the announcement would bring him running . . . and that mistake she had rectified as soon as she realized it. Had it been a mistake to urge Jessica to leave town rather than wait for Ritchie to return and blast her with his anger? Matters might have been settled much more quickly than now seemed likely, Hester thought wryly, if she had not intervened . . . one blazing row would probably have finished that marriage completely and divorce proceedings might have already been in motion.

Ritchie had come back to England to find his wife missing. Instead of relief, he felt concern and anxiety and was obviously visualizing any number of dire eventualities. Hester could tell him where Jessica was to be found and assure him that she was all right. But how to explain her part in his wife's flight without appearing in an extremely bad light at a time when she felt at risk, anyway? She was deeply worried by Ritchie's odd and unexpected concern which implied that Jessica meant more to him than she had suspected or could welcome!

She thought it very likely that he would want to visit Jessica . . . and his relief at finding her safe and well might easily be confused with a false belief that they needed each other too much to part. Hester was no longer the confident beauty of the past . . . she was too much in love and terrified of losing the little she had. She felt that a meeting between them at this stage would be quite disastrous from her point of view . . . for Jessica seemed to possess some magic quality which had kept her marriage afloat for six years on the treacherous seas of international stage and screen society.

Without knowing quite what she would achieve or how she would advise Jessica when the time came, Hester decided to spend a day in the country while the weather was still so good . . .

The long spell of warm weather had enhanced the delights of life in the country. Jessica soon felt as though she had lived most of her life at Redvers House and her lovely skin had taken on a glorious golden glow from the sun. The days passed swiftly, even pleasantly, in that quiet place so untouched by outside influences.

She could not escape the thoughts of Ritchie, of course. She was haunted by the memories of her life with him. She

wondered if he was anxious about her
— even if he wanted to find her; to tell
her that he had made a mistake, that he
missed her and wanted her back. Deep
in her heart, she knew it was a wild and
foolish hope. Time and again she was
tempted to telephone him, aching to
hear his voice . . . each time, her hand
was stilled just as she reached for the
receiver.

She knew that he must be furious
with her. Naturally enough, he hated
adverse publicity. Although he had
demanded his freedom he had expected
to attain it without fuss, quietly and
discreetly . . . and if he had approached
her differently, regretting the need to
hurt her, admitting a love for another
woman that would not be denied and
asking her to forgive and understand
and allow him to be free, Jessica would
have respected his natural preference
for a quiet divorce. But, left to
cope with her dismay and despair
as best she could while he flew off
to Cyprus without an apparent care in

the world, she had been so confused and distressed that she had blurted out the whole story to a sympathetic friend . . . only to discover the next morning that the 'friend' had swiftly contacted a journalist acquaintance. Things had been quiet on Fleet Street at the time — and Ritchie Conrad was always news. Even in the days of waning marriage and frequent divorce, the fact that the handsome, talented and very popular star was tired of one wife and wanted another could be blown up out of all proportion. To cap it all, a horrified and much besieged Jessica had not stayed to face his fury but had fled, aided and abetted by Hester Carslake who could not have realized in her warm desire to be of help that the cottage she offered was scarcely habitable.

Having seen the cottage for herself, Jessica fully appreciated Gavin's indignation with her confusion between the properties. She also understood why he had been unable to allow her to leave the comfort and security of Redvers House for the doubtful accommodation offered by Brook Cottage. Jessica was still convinced that Hester had not known that the cottage was rapidly falling into disrepair and so she remained grateful to the woman who had been so generous with practical help.

She knew she should contact Hester and explain that she was staying with the Brices instead of using the cottage. But she had not yet done so. She could ask Hester to be discreet, of course . . . but that would imply a need for discretion that would lead to natural curiosity. Hester was only human — and she might let fall an inadvertent remark to someone who would misconstrue the presence of Ritchie Conrad's wife beneath Gavin Brice's roof. Whether or not one believed in the truth of Gavin's reputation, it did exist, Jessica thought ruefully . . . and people were so eager to think the worst! She dreaded a second invasion of her privacy by the press — and she shrank from involving Gavin in any unpleasant publicity.

He was working long hours in the studio, not always busy with Jessica's portrait for that was not his way and he was preparing for an exhibition of his work that was planned for the late summer. So Jessica had only been required to sit for him for two brief periods and his manner had been so impersonal and his attention so concentrated on the canvas that her earlier anxiety was allayed and even seemed absurd in retrospect. She wondered if nervous tension had caused her to imagine that he was about to kiss her . . . and she chose to forget the leaping response to him that she had experienced that day.

She spent her days just as she pleased. She basked in the sun, read a little, slept a little, wandered about the garden, listened to music and played a few bars herself on the lovely old piano that both Gavin and Rosa could play so well . . . and went back to basking in the sun. She helped Rosa with the necessary domestic chores . . . but even Rosa did little more than work at her illustrating in between bouts of sun-worshipping for such weather could not be ignored and might not last much longer.

Jessica liked to watch Rosa at work, fascinated by the skilful, rapidly executed little drawings which told a story without woe. She envied the talent that both the Brices possessed in such measure and she could not help feeling that her own life was very empty and, so far, quite pointless for all the travel and excitement and glamour that had attached to it in the past.

She felt deeply grateful towards the Brices, brother and sister. She knew that they were seeing her through a very difficult time, helping her without making it obvious . . . and she also knew that without them she would have been cast into utter despair and might easily have been tempted into doing something very foolish. She had fortunately found a new security to replace the one she had lost . . . and she did not ask herself how much longer she could rely on it.

She was unaware that she was cocooned in the shock of losing Ritchie. But Gavin Brice did and it was for this reason that he said nothing to her about leaving Redvers House, making a new life for herself . . . in fact, did not even mention his knowledge of her personal affairs and warned Rosa to behave just as though Jessica Conrad was a much-valued friend who had come to spend a few weeks with them. Fortunately, Rosa had taken one of her warmly impulsive likings to the woman. Indeed, they were great friends and might easily have known each other for years. But Rosa liked everyone — well, almost everyone, he amended wryly, recalling that his sister had seemed incapable of any kind of rapport with Hester. Of course, Hester had never cared much for Rosa, quite failing to appreciate that the natural candour of her impulsive tongue was not born of a malicious enjoyment of another's discomfiture.

Hester was inevitably in his thoughts that week for Jessica Conrad was an insistent reminder of an episode in his life that he preferred to forget . . .

He had known for a long time that Hester had simply been a fever in his blood and that they had both been spared a disastrous marriage. Nor had he ever cherished any illusion that she cared for him, knowing that her sudden desire to marry him played some mysterious part in a cold and careful calculation. It had been no surprise when she ended their engagement as abruptly as she had manoeuvred its existence . . . but it had been a painful jolt to his pride. More than that, he had been bitterly disappointed for he had been wild to possess her, like many another man before him. He was a proud man and he realized that he had been used . . . and he resented that fact. Having finally decided to bestow the accolade of his name on a woman it had been an intolerable experience to learn that she preferred a man of Conrad's calibre. Even though he had always known instinctively that his passion for her could not last once he had possessed her, he had wanted her desperately, knowing himself to be a fool bewitched by her beauty, knowing her to be entirely without heart, ruthless and utterly selfish.

He had painted her portrait when his longing for her was at its height and he kept it in a prominent place to remind him of his vow to avoid that kind of emotional entanglement in the future. Her beauty no longer tormented him and that deceptive air of fragility no longer tugged at his emotions for he had never loved her and the flame of desire had been long extinguished. But he could not forgive the way she had used him to her own ends.

It seemed that Jessica was wholly unaware of any association between her husband and Hester. Nor did she seem to know that he had once been engaged to Hester — and that made him wonder how long and how well she had known the woman she claimed as a friend. He thought grimly that Hester was not above using a friendship with the wife as a cover for an affair with the husband and although no names had been mentioned in the press reports of the Conrad separation he thought it very likely that Hester was the woman in the case. She had told him months before with painful candour that she loved Conrad and meant to marry him.

Obviously Jessica would not have accepted the loan of Brook Cottage if she had the least idea that Hester was to blame for her unhappiness. But knowing Hester as he did, Gavin did not find it at all difficult to believe that she had contrived to get Jessica out of the way, while she cemented her position in Ritchie Conrad's life. It appeared that Jessica had been unwittingly used by Hester . . . and perhaps with the same end in view.

He had studied Jessica during the past days although she did not realize it. He had been careful to appear impersonal, almost indifferent, more concerned with his work than her affairs or state of mind. He knew that she had been relieved by Rosa's timely arrival — and he knew that the kiss that had never happened had put her very much on her guard. She would not have stayed if Rosa had not come home that day and he felt that she was thankful that it had proved possible for her to remain at Redvers House.

He noticed that she gradually relaxed and began to smile again. He was delighted when he heard her laugh quite spontaneously for the first time. Hearts did not really break, after all — but it was early days for Jessica to realize that fact. He watched as the tensions gradually fell away from her, revealing that she was little more than a girl who had been starved of the affection and attention that she desperately needed. With a spark of anger, he wondered what kind of man it was that could take a lovely, laughing girl and turn her into an anxious, sad-eyed woman whose nerves were stretched almost to breaking-point — and what kind of loving it was that had made her a willing mould for such brutal, clumsy hands?

His ready compassion had been aroused from the beginning. His incurably tender heart insisted that she needed him or someone like him to stand her friend . . . and he was determined to do all he could to restore her peace of mind and to guide her to a new way of life that would eventually heal the hurtful scars of the old . . .

8

SITTING in her car, Hester stared at the cottage in dismay and for the first time she felt a twinge of anxiety on her own account. She had not been insensitive to Ritchie's unspoken fears for his wife and now she began to wonder if there could be any foundation for them. For it was very obvious that Jessica was not using the cottage — and she was shocked to discover how dilapidated it had become in a short time.

She could visualize the blow it must have been to the overwrought Jessica to reach the place she had referred to as a 'sanctuary' only to find it virtually inhabitable. Hester tried to imagine how she must have reacted, what she would then have done, where she would have turned. But she did not really know the other woman well enough to judge.

It must have been dark when she arrived. Hester recalled that it had been an unpleasant night in London, wet and windy and unseasonably cold, and it must have been much the same in this part of the country.

She had been so sure of finding Jessica at the cottage that it was something of a shock to realize that she could never have been there at all. No one in their senses would have crossed the threshold.

There was no sign of Jessica's car, absolutely no sign of life at all. Nevertheless Hester decided she ought to make quite sure. With a faintly shrinking heart, not quite knowing what she feared, she made her way towards the door. No key was needed although she had a duplicate ... the wooden door was hanging from one hinge. Several of the windows were broken ... an upper window was hanging loosely and the curtains had been torn to shreds by wind and rain.

135

She entered gingerly . . . and retreated hastily, repelled by the damp, musty smell. The state of the place indicated that it had been used by a tramp at some time and she felt faintly indignant that Gavin had not kept an eye on the cottage for her. Then, fairly, she admitted that she had no right to expect anything from a man she had treated rather shabbily and that she was entirely to blame for the condition of the cottage. Instead of leaving it to rot, she should have completed its modernization and put it up for sale . . . such properties were bringing high prices just now and it was no great distance from London, after all. She would never want to use it again herself, of course . . . its proximity to Redvers House would be too uncomfortable for all concerned.

She and Gavin had not met in months . . . since the day she had ended their engagement, in fact. He had been justifiably angry and she had deliberately kept out of his way.

But she missed him at times for they had been friends for years before she had deliberately set out to win him as a lover, succeeding with an ease that had surprised even the confident Hester Carslake. She had meant only to make Ritchie jealous when he heard that she was running around with Gavin whose reputation with women was well-known . . . and then Gavin had played right into her hands by proposing marriage and it had seemed a much more powerful weapon in her battle to extricate Ritchie from his wife's clutches. But her engagement had proved to be an utter waste of time for Ritchie had not come running, after all . . . and it had soon proved more difficult than she had supposed to find satisfactory excuses for delaying the wedding that an impatient Gavin so much desired. Eventually she had been forced into truth . . . partly because she was too miserable without Ritchie to carry on and partly because she could not continue to stifle her conscience where Gavin was concerned.

She turned to look down the lane. Redvers House was hidden by a clump of trees but she could just see its chimneys outlined against the sky from where she stood. She had driven past the house without seeing either Gavin or his sister about and it was possible that they were both away from home. But she had been too intent on getting to Jessica to give them more than a passing thought. Now she wondered if they could possibly know anything about Jessica and her present whereabouts . . . it was the nearest house and it was possible that she had gone to it for assistance if she had seen lights, hoping for direction to the nearest town or hotel.

Hester hesitated, a little reluctant to meet Gavin. He had always been such a proud man . . . she did not suppose that he had forgiven her. He had loved her desperately, she knew . . . loving Ritchie more with every passing day, she had more understanding of the way that Gavin had felt about her and the pain she must have caused him to know. She had only to think of Ritchie sharing the daily intimacies of married life with his wife and her heart contracted with sudden anguish. It must have been a bad time for Gavin who had fallen so heavily in love and wanted her so badly only to learn that she had never intended to marry him and was desperate to belong to another man.

Memories came flooding as she sat in the car, a mere hundred yards or so from Redvers House. She recalled the day when she had finally told Gavin the truth and she remembered that he had frightened her with his anger . . . with his blue eyes blazing, a tiny nerve throbbing in his cheek and a grimness of expression that alarmed her, he had gripped her slender wrist so fiercely that she had carried the marks of his fingers for days and she would never ever forget some of the things he had said to her in that cold contemptuous fury.

It had been more than the ending of an engagement, she thought wryly. It had ended a friendship of several years standing and there were moments when she missed Gavin very much. She missed his kindness, his staunch loyalty, his swift and generous understanding and she had felt particularly secure in the warm affection which she had so stupidly misused. The kind of friendship that Gavin had given was not easily found — and not even valued properly until lost, she admitted.

Ritchie meant all the world to her . . . but Gavin was something special and suddenly she wanted very much to see him, to talk to him — if only for a little while. Impulsively, she started the car, reversed it in the lane and drove back towards Redvers House . . .

As it happened, Gavin was alone in the house for Rosa and Jessica had gone to the village to shop. Quite unable to settle to any work, he made a pot of coffee and carried the tray into the sitting-room, expecting the girls back at any moment. Hearing the car, he went to the door to help with the unloading . . . and checked at the sight of Hester, his smile of welcome fading abruptly.

She sat behind the wheel looking at him — and her own smile flickered uncertainly as she realized that he was not at all pleased to see her. She did not blame him for an obvious reluctance to pick up any threads but it hurt her nevertheless to notice his instinctive dismay.

He walked towards the car. "This is a surprise," he said slowly.

She smiled wryly. "And not a very welcome one, I see," she said with her characteristic directness. "I shouldn't have come, Gavin."

He looked down at her with a faintly quizzical expression in his very blue eyes. "Did you expect a fanfare of trumpets? You should have sent notice that you were coming to call . . . we

141

would have arranged an appropriate reception!"

"I came on impulse," she said lightly.

"You and your impulses," he told her mockingly. He returned her steady gaze with a hint of amusement lurking about his mouth. "Now I wonder what you want," he said softly, drily. He had learned the hard way that she was not to be trusted but he was curious to know what had brought her to Bednoken. She was slim and elegant and very lovely in the tailored linen suit . . . and very much aware of her beauty, he thought shrewdly. He was faintly surprised but wholly relieved to discover that she no longer had the slightest impact on his emotions.

"Why, nothing — except a cup of coffee, perhaps," she returned, smiling, encouraged by the ease of his manner and the hint of laughter in his eyes. She seized on the implication that he was willing to forgive and forget . . . and she admitted that it was very much more than she deserved.

142

Accompanying him into the house and then to the sitting-room, Hester was startled and oddly touched to discover that her portrait was still hung above the fireplace. She turned to him with a swift, warmly gratified smile. Indicating the portrait, she said with absolute sincerity: "I've always considered that to be your masterpiece, you know . . . you saw right through to the real me, didn't you?"

"Not quite soon enough, unfortunately," he returned, rather drily.

"Ouch . . . !" she exclaimed with a little laugh. "I asked for that, of course!" She sat down in a deep armchair and looked about her with a warm glow of pleasure. "It is nice to be here again," she said impulsively.

He smiled at her but he was still suspicious of her sudden and totally unexpected visit. "You timed your arrival well," he told her smoothly. "I'd just made fresh coffee."

"Telepathy?" she suggested lightly.

"Not so, I'm afraid . . . I'm expecting

Rosa. She went down to the village shops but she'll be back at any moment."

"Then I must hope to miss her," Hester said lightly. "I was never one of her favourite people and she told me so with no holds barred the last time we met!" She smiled ruefully. "She is always very quick in your defence, Gavin."

"Yes, I know." He poured coffee into two cups. "What brings you to this part of the world anyway? More than an impulse to see me, surely?"

"I've been having a look at the cottage," she told him carelessly. "It's in a very bad condition, unfortunately . . . I really had no idea!"

"I thought you must have sold the place," he said lightly.

"I'd almost forgotten all about it, to tell the truth. Then a friend asked to use it for a few days and that made me wonder what state it was in. So I came down to see . . . and I wish I'd checked before giving my friend a key to the place but obviously she took one look and ran! Heaven knows what she thought of my generosity!"

"I knew it was going to rack and ruin but I supposed you'd sold it and the new owners were only interested in developing the land eventually. It's a pity it has been so neglected, though . . . it would have been a valuable property if you'd carried out all your original plans."

"Oh, it was a short-lived enthusiasm," she admitted, shrugging. "I'm not a country-lover at heart, after all." She hesitated briefly. "I suppose you haven't seen anyone about the place lately?" she asked lightly.

It seemed a careless question but he knew his Hester . . . he realized immediately that she had driven forty miles from London for the sole purpose of finding Jessica Conrad. Failing to find her at the cottage as she had expected, she had come to him in case he had seen or spoken to her on the night of her sudden flight from town.

It was a reasonable supposition . . . the lane was little-used and led only to his house and to Brook Cottage. A passing car might have attracted his attention. It was equally likely that a stranger might call at the house for assistance and advice after discovering the cottage to be in such a deplorable condition.

He knew from the little Jessica had said that Hester had urged her to escape the attentions of the Press and to borrow the cottage so that she could spend a little time quietly on her own while she adjusted to the collapse of her marriage. Hester's primary concern in life was one of self-interest, Gavin thought cynically . . . if she had helped Jessica Conrad then she had a motive for doing so and he was highly suspicious of that motive!

He could not believe it had been easy for Hester to swallow her pride and drive up to his door — she must be very anxious to find Jessica, he thought drily. He was sure that she was no friend to Ritchie Conrad's wife and he had no intention of telling her that Jessica was at present his guest. He knew instinctively that Hester would not hesitate to make use of that piece of information, conveniently overlooking the fact of Rosa's presence as chaperone!

"I haven't been near the cottage for some weeks," he returned with truth. "But I doubt if anyone has been using it . . . except a tramp, perhaps. That did happen during the winter, I know — the local constable chased the poor devil off the premises eventually."

Hester nodded absently, frowning a little. "I dare-say my friend never came down, after all . . . people do change their minds at the last moment."

"Frequently," he agreed drily. "Women are particularly unpredictable, in my experience." He glanced at his watch, a little pointedly. He wanted her to leave before Rosa and Jessica got back but she was settled in her chair and sipping coffee with every appearance of enjoyment. Despite her declaration that she did not want to meet Rosa it looked very much as though she was waiting to see her . . . and he could scarcely hustle her from the house.

He regarded her steadily and quite dispassionately, thankful that no vestige of his former feeling for her remained. He had occasionally wondered how he would react when they met again, knowing it to be inevitable for they had many mutual friends. In recent months, those friends had been tactful but there had always been the risk of a chance meeting. He had certainly never expected her to come knocking at his door and, considering the way they had parted, he could not believe that her visit was prompted by any real desire to see him again.

Meeting his eyes, Hester did not find — as she had half-expected — that they held any lingering warmth and she felt an odd little tug of disappointment. She had not known that she valued his affection and approval so much . . . now she was taken aback to realize that she had lost both so completely. Deep down, she had believed that she had only to beckon and he would come running — and she had an instinctive reluctance to break entirely with any man who played some part in her life. One never knew what the future held, after all . . .

Gavin was really very attractive and very much a man. A rake, really — but that only added to his attractions for most women. There had been so many women in his life that she supposed it had been a terrific compliment that he had wanted to marry her. Now she thought about it, she felt that he would have made a good husband. She had never truly appreciated him during their brief engagement for her thoughts had all been of Ritchie rather than the man who imagined she meant to marry him . . . she had continued to look upon Gavin as the faithful old friend who would always be dear to her although it was impossible to love him.

If Ritchie had never existed, she might have married Gavin and been reasonably happy. There were moments when she almost wished that she had never met and loved Ritchie Conrad . . . life might have been less complicated, less demanding and less painful at times even if she had never known the height — and the depths — of loving as she did now.

Sensitive to his coolness, his anxiety to see her go, Hester knew that if Ritchie failed her — and she did not blind herself to the possibility — it would be useless to turn to Gavin for comfort and reassurance and renewed security. Whatever he had once felt for her no longer existed . . . and the realization caused her a faint pang.

She finished her coffee and set down her cup. She had come to find Jessica and she had not found her . . . and there was a faint niggle of apprehension at the back of her mind. She had called to see Gavin on a foolish impulse and he had told her without words that she no longer meant anything in his life. It had not been a very successful day, she thought wryly.

"Well, Gavin . . . it was nice to see you," she said lightly glancing at the delicate wristwatch she wore. "But I mustn't outstay my welcome . . . "

He ignored the faint mockery behind the words and rose courteously to escort her to her car, making not the slightest attempt to detain her and quite indifferent to her obvious awareness of his impatience to be rid of her.

A faintly rueful smile played about her mouth. Being the woman that she was, she found it impossible to accept that everything between them was entirely and utterly over . . . she would not accept that he could really look at her and not feel the impact of her beauty, be with her and not ache once more to hold her in his arms. Such a short time ago, he had been on fire for her . . . and surely one spark of that blazing passion must remain . . . ?

9

SHE put her hand on his arm and
looked up at him a little wistfully.
"Do you find it so hard to forgive
me, Gavin?" she asked softly.

He looked down at her warily. "You
were forgiven months ago, my dear
Hester," he said carelessly. "I'm not a
man to bear grudges as you very well
know."

"Forgiven . . . *and* forgotten?" There
was a faint challenge in her green
eyes.

"You must learn to let go, Hester,"
he told her lightly, knowing exactly
what was passing through her mind.
She did not want him, he knew . . . she
simply hated to admit that any man
could cease to want her "You hate
to believe that a door is closed, I
know," he went on, smiling. "But
you slammed it shut yourself and I've

152

learned to prefer it that way."

Hester disliked the knowledge that she was so transparent and she smarted at the ease with which he could rebuff her. But she was not the kind of woman to show anger in such a situation. Instead she laughed softly. "I wonder . . . ?" she murmured provocatively. "Was it really so easy to forget me, Gavin?"

He smiled faintly. "Very easy," he assured her, pulling no punches.

"Then you are to be envied," she returned swiftly. "For it hasn't been so easy for me — and I have tried, Gavin."

"I'm sure you have," he said drily.

She ignored the irony. "You were always very dear to me." She sighed. "I suppose it went deeper with me than with you."

Totally unmoved, he nodded. "Very likely," he agreed . . . and his eyes crinkled with laughter as he caught the faint flash of indignation in her eyes. "You didn't believe that I'd been

153

nursing a broken heart all these months, surely?"

"No, of course not . . . but there hasn't been anyone else, has there?" she challenged him swiftly. "And that isn't like you!"

He shook his head in amused incredulity. "You really are the most egotistical person I've ever known!" he exclaimed, laughing.

"And therefore quite unforgettable, darling!" she countered blithely. She smiled up at him. "Truly, I have missed you, Gavin — and I think you must have missed me a little." She moved just a little closer to him and looked up at him with a warm invitation in her green eyes. "I think I could make you love me again . . . if I chose," she murmured softly.

"But I never loved you, Hester," he told her, smiling.

Refusing to be rebuffed, she slid her arms up and about his neck and leaned against him, her lovely head tilted so that she could look into his eyes with a tantalizing promise in her own gaze. "You wanted me . . . and I could make you want me again," she whispered.

He put his arms about her slender waist and drew her closer, too much of a man not to enjoy the sensual contact of her slim and beautiful body but he knew from bitter past experience the haunting promise in eyes and lips and body was never fulfilled by the woman who used her beauty and her physical appeal to her own ends.

"You really are incredibly attractive, darling," Hester said softly, gratified to discover that he was not so immune to her attractions as he had professed. "I meant to be so cool, so distant — but all my resolutions vanished when you looked at me with just that particular smile in your eyes!"

He reproached her with laughing eyes. She was so overt, so obvious . . . and at the same time so very sure that if she had been in earnest he would have fallen for it hook, line and sinker — just as he had in the past! "Don't play off your tricks on me, Hester," he said lightly. "They won't work any more and I've learned the hard way that you aren't to be trusted!"

"But I'm not asking you to trust me," she murmured, pressing even closer to him and brushing her warm lips against his throat. "Just love me a little, Gavin . . . " Her lips strayed from his throat to the proud chin and then to the corner of his mouth — and desire leaped in him just as she had known that it would.

He kissed her fiercely and with a passion that owed nothing whatsoever to any finer feelings . . . and Jessica chose that very moment to burst into the room, flushed and breathless from hurrying, exclaiming: "Gavin — do come! The car's broken down at the corner . . . " She trailed off, astonished and embarrassed and oddly dismayed.

They broke apart. Hester stared at Jessica in equal astonishment and anger. It had been a very satisfying moment and she resented the interruption . . . more than that, it was a shock to recognize the implications of that interruption. Jessica obviously had the freedom of the house and the easy use of Gavin's name and her obvious dismay at finding him in another woman's arms told its own story. From feeling vaguely sorry for the woman, Hester swung to a swift conviction that Jessica Conrad was much more devious than anyone had ever suspected.

Gavin moved instinctively towards Jessica, a warning in his eyes which she did not understand but which did not escape Hester's shrewd notice.

"Broken down, has it?" he said lightly, endeavouring to brush aside the awkwardness of the moment. "It probably needs a good kick in the right place." He was well used to the peccadilloes of Rosa's little sports car.

He smiled down at Jessica in warm reassurance — and she experienced a sudden and alarming revelation. Her instinctive dismay at finding him in that close embrace had sprung from a fierce jealousy and her own inexplicable desire to know his kisses and the strength of his arms about her . . .

"Can you be quick?" she asked, a little diffidently. "I was just turning right into the lane and the car is stuck in the middle of the road."

"Very nasty," he agreed, smiling. "No wonder you've been hurrying in this heat. Sit down and get your breath back while I go to the rescue . . . Hester, will you give me a lift to the corner? You were just leaving, weren't you?"

"Now that I've discovered Jessica to be safe and sound there's nothing to keep me here," she agreed drily.

Jessica turned to her quickly, contrite. "Oh, Hester — I *am* sorry! I ought to have phoned! Have you been anxious? Did you come all this way just to find out what happened to me?"

"Quite unnecessarily, it appears. Never mind . . . I'm glad that you fell on your feet," Hester drawled sweetly.

Assuming that she had heard the whole story from Gavin, Jessica turned to smile at him warmly, gratefully. "I'm very fortunate in my friends," she said simply.

Hester's eyes narrowed in dislike. It was obvious that the woman was deeply involved with Gavin and she would not be surprised to learn that she had never intended to make use of the cottage but had seized on its proximity to Redvers House to deceive her and presumably others into the belief that she was there rather than consoling herself in Gavin's arms. The theatre had lost a great actress, Hester conceded drily . . . she had seemed so genuinely distressed at her husband's behaviour and yet she had already made her plans to fly to a lover for comfort and protection! Well, it suited her book . . . now she could tell Ritchie with truth that he had no need to be anxious about his wife — and Jessica had played right into their hands by so obligingly providing

Ritchie with every reason to sue for a divorce!

"If you count me as a friend then it seems a little strange that you couldn't trust me," she said in light reproach.

"I meant to let you know I was here," Jessica said quickly. "But the days have slipped by and it didn't seem terribly important. You told me to get away and put everything out of my mind for a while — and I suppose I've done just that!"

"I can see that you have," Hester said drily. She smiled unpleasantly, regarding Jessica with acute dislike, thinking of the many months of longing, of frustration and heartache, that she had caused. "Of course, if I'd known that you and Gavin were such close friends . . . " She trailed off with deliberate meaning and laughed softly. "You must be furious with me for stumbling on your secret — no one would dream of looking here for you!"

Jessica was puzzled and disturbed by

the enmity in those green eyes . . . and then she realized that Hester was hurt and angry and jealous. Gavin could not have explained, after all — and Hester had leaped to the foolish conclusion that they were more than friends. She smiled at the other woman gently, reassuringly. "You don't understand . . . " She began lightly.

Hester smiled — and it was a knowing little smile that stopped Jessica in the middle of her sentence and made her suddenly angry enough to hit her. "My dear, I understand perfectly," Hester said, a little too sweetly. "Don't think I blame you . . . after all, what's good for the gander must be equally attractive to the goose!"

"That's enough!" Gavin snapped, taking a step towards her.

"For the moment," she agreed smoothly, moving towards the door. "But I'm afraid you can't expect me to keep this to myself . . . Ritchie will be delighted to hear that his wife is safe and well and enjoying life in your arms!"

The colour drained from Jessica's lovely face. There was so much venom in those word's . . . the venom of a jealous woman who believed herself to be supplanted. "You are making a mistake," she declared involuntarily. "And Ritchie wouldn't believe it, anyway!"

Hester laughed once more . . . that soft, infuriating little laugh. "But it will suit him to believe it, Jessica. He wants out — or have you forgotten that fact during the past idyllic week?"

Jessica turned away abruptly, her expression so dismayed that Gavin's tender heart turned over. "You really are a bitch," he told Hester quietly and with cold fury. She merely smiled, not at all perturbed by the words or his anger. The confidence in that smile was almost shocking . . . and he very much regretted the stupidity of succumbing to the momentary temptation in her eyes and lips and warm body, knowing that she would go away with the firm conviction that she could have him if she chose whereas he knew without a shadow of doubt that the kiss they had exchanged had completely erased all feeling for her. He had known a fierce contempt for his own weakness and all desire had abruptly died on him while he held her in his arms. It was most unfortunate that Jessica had witnessed that meaningless embrace . . . even more unfortunate that Hester had not only discovered that Jessica was his guest but had also chosen to put entirely the wrong construction on the circumstances. He knew that she would not hesitate to make mischief . . .

"I've always found that if one wants something badly enough one gets it . . . in the end," Hester said lightly. "Sometimes one has to be a little ruthless . . . " She shrugged. She glanced towards Jessica's slim back and her eyes hardened. She might consider it convenient that Ritchie's wife had promptly found consolation in another man's arms but she was too feminine to be pleased that it should be Gavin. She did not want him herself just now but she preferred to know that he was available if she should change her mind. "Most of us take what we want, after all," she added silkily. "And you always did have a preference for other men's wives, darling."

Before he could speak or move, she swept from the room and out of the house . . . and Gavin did not go after her. Instead he crossed the room to Jessica and laid an arm about her shoulders, giving her a reassuring little hug.

She looked up at him, touched by his swift understanding and the warm sympathy in that gesture. "It's all right," she said simply. "It's just that . . . well, I thought she was a friend. Suddenly she hates me — but I think I understand that. She didn't expect me to be here — and I couldn't have chosen a worse moment to announce my presence. I'm so sorry, Gavin."

"You don't have to apologize to me," he told her, smiling. "You were a welcome interruption . . . but we'll talk about that later. I must go and rescue poor Rosa, you know . . ."

"Don't bother! Poor Rosa has been rescued by a handsome young man in a Rolls Royce," his sister announced blithely from the doorway. "It was just as well he turned up, obviously." She sat down and looked expectantly from one to the other. "Well — I'm all agog! Tell me what I've missed!! What was Hester doing here — and in *such* a temper! She almost ran me down and she was extremely rude about my driving!"

"Is the car all right?" Gavin asked evasively.

"Thanks to Sir Galahad it goes again — and, no thanks to Miss Hester Carslake, it has a deep scratch along the wing. She was in a hurry to get away, wasn't she? Did you have a lovely quarrel, Gavin?" she asked gleefully.

He frowned. "I'd like to wring her neck," he said with feeling.

"Well, that's nothing new," she retorted blithely.

"I must have a look at the car," he said.

"Do — and get the groceries out of the back for me would you?" Rosa called after him. She sat back and smiled at Jessica. Then, noticing the abstraction in those grey eyes, she said lightly: "You want to forget any nasty remarks that Hester might have made, you know . . . she's never happy unless she's making someone squirm!" She reached for a cigarette. "I wonder what she wanted . . . nothing good, I expect. I'm surprised that Gavin didn't murder her and bury her body in the garden while he had the place to himself!"

Jessica could not muster an answering smile. Without looking at Rosa, she said stiffly: "I don't think he was feeling murderous, as it happens."

"Oh . . . ?" Rosa was instantly struck by a certain inflection in her tone. "I hope that doesn't mean they've kissed and made up!"

"I think they were on the verge of it . . . she certainly wasn't at all pleased when I barged in at a tender moment," Jessica commented wryly. "She leaped to all the wrong conclusions and wouldn't listen to any explanations . . . and I'm sure that she means to make trouble."

"Let her try . . . " Rosa said carelessly.

"But you don't understand," Jessica said swiftly. "She said that Ritchie . . . my husband — that he will be very interested to know that I'm here — oh, you must know what she was implying, Rosa? I don't need to spell it out, surely? And Ritchie will believe it because it will suit him to believe it — Hester said that and I'm afraid that it's true."

"Oh, she's an unpleasant piece of work but I'm sure you've no need to worry," Rosa said gently, reassuringly. "The mere fact that two people have shared the same roof isn't very good evidence for a divorce court . . . and that's what you fear, isn't it?"

"If the case never came to court the mud would still stick," Jessica said unhappily. "People always want to believe the worst."

"But if you are innocent . . . " Rosa began — and broke off, a little self-conscious, as she met the faint reproach in Jessica's quick glance.

"You see . . . even you are not sure," Jessica said quietly, ruefully. "I don't think you know what to believe."

It was true. Rosa had instinctively leaped to the defence of her brother and this woman of whom she had become very fond. But in her heart she did not know what to believe about their relationship. She had not asked any questions and they had said very little. Gavin seemed a little distant with Jessica at times . . . and oddly tender and protective towards her at other times. Rosa was convinced that some kind of rapport existed between them and realized that circumstances must make it very difficult for them to publicize their feelings.

She did not know how long or how well they had known each other or if Gavin could be blamed in any way for the collapse of Jessica's marriage. She had never seen any real evidence that they were lovers — if it was so they were behaving with remarkable circumspection at the moment.

At first dismayed, she had come to feel that Jessica might suit her brother very well once she was free of a disastrous marriage. But it was obvious that two proud people — and they were both proud — would never allow a public scandal to force them together even if they wanted each other more than anything else in the world!

Life could be very complicated, she thought wryly. Thank heavens she knew exactly where she stood with

Brent and knew that one day they would slip easily and inevitably into a marriage that would bring them both the happiness that had so far eluded them . . .

10

AT her first opportunity, Jessica slipped out into the garden, needing a few minutes to herself. Rosa was very kind but she could not be expected to understand the turmoil of thought and feeling that she was experiencing.

It had been a shock to learn that the woman she supposed to be her friend could contemplate wreaking havoc with her life. She could understand that Hester was consumed with jealousy . . . obviously she was still in love with Gavin and had swallowed her pride to seek him out only to find that he was entertaining another woman. She had leaped to all the wrong conclusions, of course and had been in no mood to listen to explanations. Jessica wondered if she would really carry out that threat to tell Ritchie a tissue of lies. He would certainly seize on the kind of information she had to offer, she thought wryly . . . anxious for his freedom, he would not hesitate to cite a man he did not know and had no reason to consider!

Jessica was aware that Gavin had been involved in other scandals . . . hence his reputation. But she felt quite sick with apprehension at the thought that he might be dragged unwillingly into the mess of her marriage. For herself, she did not care what happened . . . somehow, she no longer cared what Ritchie did to hurt and humiliate her. He would get his freedom one way or another, she knew — he always did get what he wanted. But she could not allow Gavin to be penalized simply because he had shown her kindness and compassion.

She found herself by the open door of the studio. Without consciously thinking about it, she went in and looked about her, absorbing the atmosphere.

She did not need Gavin's physical

presence to be very much aware of him . . . the vitality, the strength of character, the temperament and the essential goodness of the man who had impressed this place so much with his personality. Something deep within her being stirred abruptly and a little painfully. It was an odd sensation . . . a kind of yearning that defied description. For the moment she did not recognize it as the awakening of an instinctive need for all that Gavin Brice could offer a woman. It was a deep-rooted ache, a sense of longing, the insistent need to belong entirely and eternally to one man who would love her as she needed to be loved. It owed little at that moment to the physical desire which he could cause to leap so swiftly and alarmingly — and yet she was woman enough to know that sex must play its part in every relationship, however subtly, however innocently.

Her portrait was on its easel, paint and palette thrown down close by. The canvas was not covered for he had been working that morning and left it abruptly. Jessica's eyes widened in surprise as she realized the perfection of the almost-finished work. She had not known that he was making such progress . . . he had implied that there were weeks of work to be done before he would be satisfied with the portrait and he had carefully concealed the canvas from her, explaining that he disliked to show his work in a half-finished state.

It was a full-length canvas . . . showing the girl that was herself as the artist saw her — young, appealingly lovely but lost and bewildered, wreathed in the mists of confusion, stretching out a hand to anyone who would help her, show her the way. In a corner of the canvas was an open door and beyond it the radiance of new hope, new life, new happiness. But the tears that welled and overspilled were apparently blinding the lost girl to the existence of that door . . .

Jessica thrilled to the symbolism of

the portrait . . . and she was humbled by the magnificence, the beauty, the purity of its significance and its skill. Here was the work of a great artist . . . and a great man.

Gavin paused in the doorway — and Jessica turned quickly. Seeing him, she smiled. There was so much sweetness, so much warmth, so much trust in the smile which reached her eyes . . . and in that moment Gavin knew that he loved her. It was no bolt from the blue as the poets claimed . . . merely a quiet acceptance of an inevitable truth that had been making itself felt in his life since the first moment of meeting this woman.

He believed in destiny, knowing that all of life has its pattern and that every incident, however trivial it might seem, wove a new thread into that pattern. He was wholly convinced that Jessica had come into his life through an accident that was no accident but part of the design that made up both their lives.

He had no way of knowing if destiny meant them to find happiness together or if he only had a small part to play in her life. Perhaps he was only meant to help her through a difficult time without gaining any personal satisfaction from their brief contact. The love she had inspired might merely be meant to provide her with a security that she temporarily needed . . . he could not know if she was meant to love him in return. If it was meant to be, it would happen. Love — and time's healing power — could work miracles. For the moment she was still deeply in love with her husband, he thought wryly — and knew he must accept the pain of that knowledge as part of loving. He had been born to love Jessica, to do what he could to help her regain the peace of mind that she had lost . . . and he must try to ignore the selfish clamouring of his own needs and desires.

"Gavin . . . I haven't any words," she said simply, holding out her hand to him.

He took that outstretched hand and clasped it very tightly, struggling with the emotions she invoked simply by being there, so near and yet so terribly out of his reach. "I gather that you are pleased," he said lightly.

"It's quite beautiful," she murmured . . . and realized that her heart was behaving in a most alarming manner as he stood beside her, studying the canvas, her hand firmly clasped in his own. "I ought not to have peeked, I know," she added, a little breathlessly, "but I couldn't resist the temptation."

"What woman could, I wonder?" he teased gently.

He smiled down at her with a certain warmth in his very blue eyes . . . and suddenly her heart seemed to be taking flight. She was lost in those blue depths, quite forgetful of everything but the magnetism of this man's warm and vibrant personality, every fibre of her being aware of wanting him . . .

Gavin dropped her hand and busied himself with covering the canvas, abruptly breaking the spell — not because he suspected the tumult within her but because the longing to take her into his arms and hold her close to his heart had become almost intolerable.

"I'm quite proud of it," he admitted with a casualness that did not deceive Jessica. "I hope to show it at the Academy next year. It isn't finished, of course . . . it needs a few touches yet."

"But you no longer need me to sit for you," she pointed out, a little too swiftly. She had suddenly realized the full danger of remaining at Redvers House. She had supposed it to be merely a matter of finding him rather too attractive for any woman's peace of mind . . . particularly a woman in her position. Never in her wildest dreams had she visualized the possibility of falling headlong in love with him . . . but she knew only too well that she was on the verge of doing that very thing. She must go away before she did anything so foolish. She felt that she had suffered enough heartache and humiliation without inviting more by loving again . . . no, not again, she amended honestly, knowing at last that her youthful obsession with Ritchie had never resembled the kind of loving that should exist between man and woman.

It would be the height of folly to allow herself to love Gavin Brice, she told herself as firmly as she could . . . for one thing, it did not seem as though his affair with Hester had really ended . . . for another, his reputation where women were concerned could not lead any woman to suppose that his emotions were deep or lasting. Most important of all, she was not free to love any man but her husband . . . even though that husband neither loved nor wanted her any more.

Gavin paused and turned to look at her steadily. "Getting restless, Jessica?" he asked quietly. "You must be bored, of course . . . you are used to a very different way of life."

"I'm not bored," she disclaimed swiftly. "It's just . . . well, I left town in a hurry and there are things I didn't do. I ought to go back and sort them out. I'm very grateful to you and Rosa . . . you've both been wonderful. But I really mustn't impose on your generosity any longer . . ." She trailed off, meeting the laughter in his eyes.

He smiled, the warmth of understanding in his voice as he said softly: "Trying to protect me, Jess?"

Faint colour stole into her lovely face. "I don't want you involved," she admitted without any further attempt at prevarication. He was too shrewd, too sensitive . . . and he seemed to know her much too well for comfort, she thought ruefully.

"My shoulders are very broad," he assured her carelessly.

"That isn't the point!" she exclaimed warmly. "You can't want to be cited in a divorce case when you've done nothing! I don't think you realize that

Ritchie has no scruples . . . and no conscience!"

He shrugged. "I can be unscrupulous myself," he told her lightly. Abruptly he tilted her face with strong fingers beneath her chin, forcing her to meet the eyes that held a hint of laughter. "If he hangs the name on me I might be very tempted to earn it," he said softly.

Taken aback, scarcely daring to believe that it was anything more than a joke in rather doubtful taste, Jessica took refuge in flippancy. "You would need a certain amount of co-operation, you know. And I learned a long time ago that it's a mistake to offer the slightest encouragement to any man with your kind of reputation!" The words and tone were light and teasing but he released her immediately and she had the oddest impression that she had hurt him.

Gavin knew that he had nearly betrayed the way he felt about her . . . and he knew, too, that the rebuke, delivered so lightly, was well-deserved. He had briefly forgotten that despite everything she was still in love with her husband and that she was naturally dreading the very thought of being divorced by him on any grounds whatsoever. It was a mistake to regard the matter as lightly as he did, his optimism leaping ahead to a future day when she would be a free woman and might be willing to look on him as a lover as well as a friend.

"Let's be serious about this," he said abruptly. "You appear to think that Conrad will accept any lies that Hester chooses to tell him . . . and we both know what she has threatened to tell him. So you are obviously aware of their relationship . . . " He broke off as a little exclamation flew from her lips and stared incredulously at her dismayed and obviously astonished face. "You did know that Hester wants your husband and means to have him, surely?" he demanded in surprise.

"Hester . . . and Ritchie?" She shook

her head in utter disbelief. "Oh no . . . you are mistaken! It can't be so . . ."

"It is so," he told her with quiet conviction. "I knew it months ago."

"But Ritchie has never liked her . . . he hardly knows her, in fact!"

"You are either very trusting . . . or incredibly naïve," he said wryly. "When Hester broke our engagement she told me that she meant to marry Ritchie Conrad . . . and when I reminded her that he already had a wife she said that she had not forgotten it but he had!" He saw that she winced and he added quickly, contritely: "That hurts . . . forgive me, Jess! But you have to know the truth. And it isn't the first time he's let you down, is it?"

Her mouth twisted in sudden bitterness. "I thought it was . . . so I suppose I *have* been too trusting and ridiculously naïve!" She was silent for a moment, trying to reconcile Hester with the image of the supposedly unknown woman who had taken Ritchie so completely from her. Then she said angrily: "He told me that there was someone else . . . just that — someone else. How could I have known he meant Hester? She's my friend. She was the only one who understood . . . she was kind, sympathetic . . . " She broke off. Abruptly she went to the window and stared at the garden, its radiant loveliness in the spring sunshine hurting her just a little with its beauty. "People are so hateful — such hypocrites . . . " she said unsteadily.

Gavin crossed the floor to stand behind her, raised his hand to touch the little curl that had escaped from the neat knot on the nape of her neck. "Not all of us, Jess . . . "

She shivered as his fingers brushed her neck. Abruptly she turned to him . . . and his arms were ready to receive and enfold her. She cried like a child . . . the tears welling and coursing down her cheeks, the gasping sobs coming from deep within her — and they were the healing tears that she had

184

denied herself too long.

Gavin knew that any shoulder would have sufficed in that moment . . . that he was not a man to her then but just another human being offering the comfort she needed. He held her close and stroked her hair and murmured the little soothing nonsenses that came instinctively to his lips.

Neither knew the exact moment when the relationship between them subtly altered from that of comforter and comforted. But suddenly they were man and woman and very much aware of each other as such . . . and all other considerations were forgotten. Hearts pounding, bodies straining for an even closer embrace, desire welling in a swift flood, their lips met and clung. Time stood still while the incredible magic held them both spellbound . . . weak and willing, Jessica surrendered to his kiss, content to throw all caution to the four winds . . .

Then, abruptly, forcefully, she thrust him away, finding just enough resolution to do so before she was utterly lost. "No . . . !" she cried. "No . . . !"

He captured the slender hands that pushed against his broad chest, carried them both to his lips — lips that burned with the urgency of longing. "Why not . . . who gets hurt?" he asked softly, persuasively.

She wrenched away her hands. "I do — and I *won't* be hurt any more!"

That piteous wail brought swift and tender compassion to his eyes. He checked the words with strong fingers laid gently over her lips. "I won't hurt you, darling . . . not now, not ever," he told her quietly and meant the words as he had never meant anything in his life. "You're so lovely, Jessica — so very lovely." He looked down at her with his heart in his eyes. "I want you very much . . . "

She turned away in order to strengthen her resolution. She was so meltingly weak before the warmth and the magnetism of this man's personality . . . she was so ready to love him, to give herself completely to the enchantment of his embrace. But she must keep her head . . . for this was a man who had loved many women if only half the stories told about him were true — and only a short time before she had surprised him with Hester Carslake in his arms.

"Please — don't touch me!" she exclaimed involuntarily as he put a hand on her shoulder. His hand fell . . . and fearing that she had hurt him, she turned swiftly and said impulsively: "Don't think that I don't want you, Gavin . . . I *do*! But I can't cope just yet with the way you make me feel! It's too soon . . . too sudden! You must give me more time . . . "

She broke off as Rosa appeared in the doorway. "Jess — Gavin . . . " She hesitated, reluctant to impart bad news and realizing that she had broken in on an obviously emotional scene.

"What is it?" Gavin was a little curt, wishing his sister anywhere else at that particular moment. Then, noticing her expression, he said swiftly: "What's wrong . . . what's happened?"

"I just turned on the radio for some music and caught the tail end of a news bulletin. I'm sorry, Jess — but the announcer was talking about your husband." She noticed that Gavin's hand instinctively sought Jessica's and gripped it reassuringly and that the woman turned equally instinctively towards him and her heart sank for both of them. She went on swiftly: "He has been rushed to the London Clinic after collapsing with a heart attack . . . I thought you ought to know right away."

Jessica stared, too stunned to speak. All the blood drained slowly from her cheeks. She seemed to be all enormous stricken eyes in a small, pinched face as she looked from Gavin to his sister in shocked dismay.

"I must go to him," she said in a voice that was little more than a whisper.

"I'll take you," Gavin announced firmly. "You won't want to be alone . . . and you won't feel like driving, anyway."

She nodded. "Thank you," she said dully. "I'll go and pack . . . "

She drew her hand away, scarcely aware that it had been held in his firm clasp or that she had been drawing on his strength during those first shocked moments. She hurried from the studio and down the length of the garden to the house . . . and at a nod from her brother Rosa went after her to help with the packing and maintain a steady flow of cheerful reassurances.

Jessica made little response but she was thankful for the company that forced her to keep calm, to concentrate on packing her case and to stop herself from anticipating the worst. It was impossible not to be anxious and alarmed but at least she need not cast herself into widow's weeds, she rebuked herself sternly — and reminded herself that Ritchie was already receiving expert attention and that virtual miracles were achieved in modern medicine . . .

11

JESSICA descended the narrow staircase, very composed and very beautiful, her hair coiled in its usual neat chignon, her eyes and mouth very grave.

She was so lovely that it hurt Gavin to look at her, knowing that he would never own her. Because she had been briefly swept off her feet by a very human response to his passion, he had stupidly supposed that he could teach her to love him one day . . . yet he had known from the very beginning that only one man existed for Ritchie Conrad's wife.

He moved forward to take her case. "I've been trying to telephone for you but there must be a fault on the line," he told her. "We'll try again on the way to town." He smiled down at her gently. "I'm sure you needn't be too anxious, Jess . . . he's in very good hands, you know."

She nodded. "I must go to him," she said simply, just as she had said before. She turned as Rosa came down the stairs to join them. "Thank you," she said to her. "Thank you for everything."

Rosa hugged her impulsively. "Come back as soon as you can," she invited warmly. "Don't forget that we're friends, Jess."

"I won't forget you," Jessica promised . . . but both Gavin and Rosa noticed that she did not promise to return and both were aware that it was very unlikely that she would.

The car ate up the miles, handled by a fast and skilful driver. Jessica sat silent and tense, much more consumed with a sense of guilt than a sense of foreboding. For she could not believe that Ritchie would die — he was a young man and there had never been any suspicion of heart trouble or any other illness in the past. He had probably been working too hard — and he had obviously been through a period of emotional stress before reaching the decision to ask for a divorce. And, for all she knew, he might have returned from Cyprus with a change of heart and been terribly distressed and anxious to find her gone from the flat.

She blamed herself for running away so impetuously . . . for all she knew, Ritchie might have gone through hell wondering and worrying about her during the last few days and perhaps his anxiety had brought on this heart attack.

She was consumed with guilt when she realized the disloyalty of her ready response to the attractions of the man by her side. She told herself that she had merely sought some consolation for her heartache, some balm for her bitterness . . . and perhaps a petty revenge for Ritchie's desire for another woman. But it had gone deeper than that and it would be difficult to tear it out although she must do so. For it had been very foolish and very wrong to allow herself to want any man but her husband . . . even more wrong to encourage and enjoy the strength of his arms and the urgency of his kisses. She could never forgive herself . . . or cease to make amends.

Ritchie must get well and he would need her more than ever and perhaps this was a golden opportunity to create a happier and more settled marriage. His passion for that other woman would all be forgotten she told herself confidently . . . and she was determined to put Gavin Brice right out of her mind and heart once she was back with Ritchie . . .

Ritchie Conrad was very ill, weak and shaken by the onslaught of a heart attack that had taken him completely by surprise. He was prepared to regard it as a warning and had already made up his mind to take greater care of himself and to lead a less strenuous life in future.

He was in a very chastened mood

when Jessica arrived . . . feeling that he had come very close to explaining himself to his Maker and much alarmed by the experience, he welcomed the tender concern which did not allow him even to hint at the emotional atmosphere of their last meeting.

Jessica behaved as though nothing had ever been said about another woman or his desire for a divorce . . . and Ritchie was glad to leave it at that for the time being. His sudden illness had not destroyed his feeling for Hester but desire was temporarily abated and he could think about her almost dispassionately. He marvelled that he had come so near to ending his marriage for her sake and even felt some degree of guilt that he had hurt and humiliated Jessica. She was a good, sweet girl who had never uttered a word of reproach although heaven knew he had not been a good husband to her . . .

He was content to bask in the warmth of her affection and concern and to accept her assurances that she was with him and would stay with him and he could be quite sure nothing would happen to him while she was there. Feeling very much like a frightened and very insecure child, it did not occur to him that her attitude was maternal rather than loverlike because it was exactly the kind of solicitous attention that he needed.

Jessica could not stay long for he was under intensive care and too sedated for conversation but she left him with the assurance that she would be back later. She talked to the specialist in charge of his case and learned that her husband was already on the road to recovery and a second attack was not thought to be likely as long as he slowed the hectic pace of his life.

Gavin met her as she turned away from the specialist and she hesitated in surprise. "Oh . . . I didn't know you meant to wait!" she exclaimed, smiling at him warmly in her relief.

"How is he?" he asked, knowing the

answer by her bearing and expression. He had decided to wait in the eventuality that she might need him if Conrad's condition was worse than she expected.

"Much better than I supposed . . . but he's very ill, of course," she added hastily. "It will be weeks before he can lead anything like a normal life and I shall have to take very good care of him in the future."

Gavin nodded, silencing the instinctive protest of his heart with the curt reminder that he had not expected anything but this subtle indication that whatever had been stirring to life between them must be suppressed and forgotten. He realized only too clearly that it was love and not merely duty that had brought her hotfoot to her husband's side and would keep her there for as long as she was needed. He must not wish for it to be any other way — but he was only human and he loved her and it was not easy to relinquish her without a word even though he had no right to the woman who was another man's wife.

"We must get you out of here," he said abruptly, taking her arm and guiding her along the corridor to a lift. "Perhaps now I can persuade you to eat something . . . you missed lunch, remember." She had refused to stop during the drive to London and he had not insisted, aware of her anxiety and fully understanding her need to be with her husband as soon as humanly possible.

"I'm not hungry," Jessica said, rather limply. She suddenly felt the utter exhaustion of reaction. She was glad of Gavin's supporting hand beneath her elbow. She looked up at him gratefully — but he was not looking at her and his profile seemed a little stern — handsome enough to catch at her heart but stern. Emotion welled abruptly and she caught her underlip in her teeth in dismay as she silently confessed to a desperate longing to stand in the comforting circle of his arms and forget everything but her need of him. She knew it was wrong and not at all the right time or place for such feelings — but somehow it *felt* right to want him, to want to belong to him, to want to be loved and looked after by him for the rest of her life.

She was tired and emotionally drained or she would not be feeling so foolishly, dangerously weak, she told herself . . . at the first opportunity she must send Gavin away and begin to stand on her own feet. It would be too easy to take advantage of his liking and admiration and admitted desire for her . . . and it would not be fair when she was not free to give him anything in return. But for the moment she was very glad to have him by her side and to know that she could rely on his kindness, his good nature and his willingness to smooth her path.

He had brought her to London safely and speedily and shepherded her through the host of waiting reporters with a brusque appeal to their compassion.

Now he took her out of the building by a side door, obviously by arrangement, and into the waiting car . . . and she was thankful to escape the eager attentions of the Press. Fleetingly she wondered what those reporters would make of her return to town in the company of so well-known a personality as Gavin Brice — and she made a mental note to ensure that the newspapers were kept away from Ritchie for the time being. She did not want him angered or distressed by innuendoes about her relationship with Gavin.

She could not help being thankful that if Ritchie had to have a heart attack it had happened before Hester Carslake could reach him with a false explanation of his wife's presence at Redvers House. She knew herself to be innocent — indeed if not in thought and feeling — but it might have been very difficult to convince the proud and quick-tempered Ritchie that she had been no more than a guest beneath Gavin Brice's roof and efficiently chaperoned by the man's sister to boot!

Gavin took her to a restaurant owned by one of his friends . . . and to please him, she swallowed a few mouthfuls of delicious omelette and drank some excellent coffee. They talked very little but she was much aware of his sympathetic understanding and his readiness to be of help in any way whatsoever. She wondered if she would ever be able to prove her gratitude to Gavin and Rosa for all that they had done for her. She had never known the true meaning of friendship until they had entered her life . . . her heart warmed to them both and she knew she could never forget them or cease to think of them both with affection even if she never saw either of them again.

She tried to thank Gavin before he left her in the luxurious apartment . . . but he brushed aside the faltering words.

"Isn't that what friendship is all about?" he said, smiling down at her. "Besides, I've really done very little . . . now, you know where to find me if you want me, Jessica? I shall be staying at my Club — you have the name and the telephone number in a safe place?" She nodded. "Good!" He took one of her hands into his own and suddenly his expression was very grave. "Don't let this be good-bye . . . whatever the circumstances," he said quietly. He pressed a kiss into the palm of her hand, closed her fingers tightly over it — and turning, left her abruptly. He would not wait for the lift but disappeared through the swing doors that concealed the stairway . . . and Jessica felt suddenly bereft as his tall figure vanished from her sight.

She had loved Ritchie in a youthful, immature fashion, depending on him for happiness and peace of mind. But she had never known this utter desolation of her being at parting . . . and it was all she could do to stop herself from running after Gavin and begging him not to leave her — ever!

She suddenly discovered herself to be deeply in love with the man she had known so short a time . . . with a plummeting heart, she closed the door and stood with her back to it, struggling with her emotions. Her mouth twisted as she recalled that such a little time before she had left this flat so hurriedly and in such distress, quite convinced that her heart was broken and life not worth the living without Ritchie. Now she no longer loved and wanted Ritchie — and life truly would be desolate without even the hope of sharing some part of it with Gavin Brice.

Pulling herself together, she carried her case through to the bedroom and began to unpack, returning her clothes to their former places in chest and wardrobe with a heavy heart. Many of her things were exactly as she had left them, reminding her that she had been away a very short time — and yet so much had happened.

It was hard to realize that this was the home she had shared and would presumably share again with Ritchie . . . if one could call it a home, she thought wryly, thinking of the warmth and inner serenity and quiet security that had surrounded her at Redvers House and how much she already missed it. Her heart shrivelled at the thought of the future. But she knew that there was no choice open to her . . . Richie was ill and he needed her and she was his wife.

She loved Gavin. She wanted and needed him with every fibre of her being. But he could play no part in her life except as a friend . . . and even that would present difficulties when Ritchie learned that she included the artist among her friends.

Inevitably Ritchie would learn from one source or another that she had been at Redvers House — she must contrive to give the impression that it had been Rosa Brice who befriended her and offered hospitality and that her brother's presence had been merely incidental. She shrank from the thought of playing the part of loving wife when her heart was not in it but she knew that she must not give Ritchie any cause for suspicion or jealousy. She could only hope that his inborn egotism would not allow him to suppose that she could find any man more interesting or more attractive than her husband . . .

Stepping out into the bright sunshine, Gavin checked as a car turned through the gates and approached the entrance where he stood. His eyes narrowed as he recognized the motorist and his mouth tightened a little grimly. As the car came to a halt he moved to intercept the woman behind the wheel.

Hester stared at him in pure astonishment, scarcely believing his presence in this part of the world when she had left him at Redvers House earlier in the day.

"Well met, Hester," he said lightly.

"Gavin . . . ?" she queried almost

incredulously. "What on earth . . . where did you spring from?"

"I brought Jessica back to town. I couldn't let her travel alone, in the circumstances."

Abruptly her mouth and eyes hardened. "Oh, I see . . . you persuaded her to come back!"

"There was no question of persuasion," he said tautly. "She was very anxious to see her husband . . . "

"To get in before I did, you mean?" she broke in mockingly. "What's the matter — did the game become too serious, suddenly — too much of a threat? Surely you don't suppose that you can stop me, darling . . . I mean to have Ritchie Conrad, you know!" Her chin tilted and her eyes blazed defiance at him.

It was Gavin's turn to stare at her in amazement . . . and his lip curled in contempt that she could think only of herself and her desires at such a time. "No doubt . . . but even you must realize that this is no time to be talking scandal, my dear Hester," he said drily. "When Conrad is over this crisis then you can settle matters between . . . "

"Crisis?" she interrupted fiercely, suddenly very pale. "What crisis? What do you mean?"

He looked down at her steadily. "Haven't you heard that he is very ill?"

Even her lips were white . . . and she put out a hand instinctively as though to ward off the impact of his words. "Ritchie . . . ill? No! I don't believe it! He's fine . . . I was with him only yesterday!"

"He had a heart attack this morning," he told her gently. "He's in the London Clinic . . . out of danger now but still very ill, apparently. Rosa heard the news over the radio — just after you left this morning, actually. I brought Jessica to town as soon as we knew . . . we must have passed you on the road."

"I broke my journey to lunch with some friends," she said numbly. Then she exclaimed passionately: "If Ritchie is ill then he will want me . . . you did say he was in the London Clinic?"

He checked her as she fumbled with the car keys. "Hester, you won't be allowed to see him, you know . . . not for a few days at least."

She looked up at him with very real anguish in her eyes, his words reminding her that she had no claim on Ritchie, no right to insist on being with him at a time when he must surely need her. "Not see him . . . " she echoed blankly. "But I must . . . I have to see him!"

"I can't prevent you from trying, of course — but I'm afraid you will be disappointed," he warned her kindly. "He's in the Intensive Care Unit and even Jessica could only be with him for a few minutes."

"He really is . . . *so* ill?" she asked, a little fearfully.

"They need to watch him very carefully for a little while," he temporized.

She hesitated. Then she said awkwardly: "You don't know what passed between them, I suppose ... Ritchie and Jessica?" She uttered a painful little sound that was half-laugh, half-sob. "I mean ... the circumstances are unusual, aren't they? I daresay she is the last person Ritchie wants around him but stupid convention decrees that she must rush to his bedside and pretend to care that he is ill!"

"No pretence about it!" Gavin said, a little sharply. "She does care ... just as much as you do and maybe rather more! I know it doesn't suit your plans to believe it but there's more to that marriage than you realize and six years together isn't lightly tossed aside."

He voiced a persistent fear that had haunted her for months and her heart sank. But she was too proud to show dismay. She smiled up at him ... a bold, glittering smile. "You may be right. Perhaps we are both going to be losers ... in which case, we shall have to comfort each other."

He was not deceived by the flippancy. She was frightened and anxious, more emotionally involved with Conrad that he had supposed. But so involved that she could not be persuaded to forget him? He doubted it . . . and it suddenly occurred to him that he would be helping Jessica in a very tangible way if he contrived to remove the main obstacle to her future happiness with her husband.

"It may come to that," he agreed lightly.

"Must you make it sound like a fate worse than death?" she countered coquettishly, responding as he had known that she would to the merest hint of his continued susceptibility to her charms. "Are you staying in town?"

"For a few days."

"At your club?"

"Yes."

"Then we shall see something of each other," she said confidently . . . and drove away with a careless wave of her hand.

He looked after her thoughtfully, trying to reconcile himself to the task he had set himself, trying to recall what it was that had originally caused him to suppose himself in love with that beautiful but utterly selfish young woman . . .

12

SEDATIVES ensured that Ritchie did little more than sleep for the next few days but he wanted and expected Jessica to be within reach during his waking moments. It was arranged that she should occupy a suite on the same floor and so she scarcely left the Clinic except for a brief walk in the fresh air and even then felt that she ought to hurry back in case Ritchie woke and wanted her. It was a strange, demanding existence and she soon felt as though her every nerve was being stretched to its fullest extent. Ordinary thought, ordinary emotion seemed suspended ... every moment of her life revolved around Ritchie and this new, clinging dependence in his attitude towards her.

He was making progress — and that was all that really mattered. Within a week he was feeling well enough to talk of a long holiday in Spain or Italy or the South of France as soon as the doctors agreed to it. Jessica encouraged him for she wanted to put as many miles as possible between herself and the likelihood of a chance meeting with Gavin Brice. The longing for him was almost more than she could bear but every day brought a greater realization of the futility of loving and wanting a man who was little more than a stranger. She had not seen him again and there had been no word from him in the intervening days . . . it was not that she had really expected him to communicate with her while her first concern must be for Ritchie but she still could not suppress a vague disappointment and dismay.

Having idly mentioned a holiday as a subject for conversation rather than with any real intention of making plans, Ritchie was surprised when Jessica took him up so promptly with the automatic assumption that she would accompany him. Always willing to drift with the tide, he allowed her to assume that his desire for a divorce was a thing of the past . . . and for the time being he was ready to forget it himself, to go on with the marriage that had suited him well enough for six years. No doubt he would feel differently once he was wholly recovered but it was easier and more pleasant to allow Jessica to suppose that he had overcome his love and longing for another woman.

Hester would never be out of his blood but he was not yet strong enough to reach out for the happiness they could know together . . . there was plenty of time and Hester would not expect him to be pressing the subject of divorce at this particular time, he told himself comfortably.

Hester did not neglect him. She sent fruit and flowers and books and telephoned every day for news of his progress. But she did not attempt to see him after that first day when she had been told, kindly but firmly, that he was too ill to receive visitors. Turning away reluctantly, filled with anxiety and dismay, she had almost collided with Jessica who had returned to be with her husband. The two women had looked at each other for a long moment. Without a word being spoken, Jessica had emphasized her rights as Ritchie's wife and Hester had conceded them — and only Hester knew what it had cost her to walk out of the building without knowing if she would ever see Ritchie again.

Recalling her insistence on discretion throughout their entire association, Ritchie was not surprised nor hurt that she did not visit him once he was well enough to see two or three of his friends. Nor did he express his natural desire to see her. It did not occur to him that Jessica might be puzzled by his apparent indifference for he was still unaware that she knew the identity of the woman for whom he had been ready to sacrifice his marriage.

Jessica was beginning to wonder if

she had dreamed the entire thing. After all, she had no actual evidence of an affair between her husband and Hester Carslake. Ritchie had never named any names and he had not referred to his earlier desire for a divorce. Perhaps he regretted the whole thing . . . perhaps it had died abruptly with that alarming heart attack.

She did not realize that for the moment Ritchie only wanted the wife who made absolutely no demands on him . . . she only knew that Ritchie was kind to her, gentle with her, even affectionate — and she was lulled into wondering if the future contained some degree of happiness for them, after all. Old habits die hard and she was still sufficiently involved with him to respond automatically to familiar overtures which hinted at regret for past behaviour and the unspoken promise of a better understanding in future.

She was thankful that he had not betrayed the slightest interest in her whereabouts or her activities during the week that she had spent out of town. As usual, he was solely concerned with himself and for once she welcomed that egotism!

It was an effort to be the woman he expected her to be, the wife he had airily dominated and carelessly taken for granted all those years. For she had altered, become a different person. In a very short time, she had matured and become aware of herself as a woman, discovered emotions and desires that had lain dormant for too long, and briefly enjoyed a degree of independence which she was now reluctant to relinquish. She had known a brief taste of freedom from the self-imposed tyranny of her marriage and now she chafed at the bonds which threatened to tighten about her once more. She marvelled at the youthful acceptance of Ritchie's careless indifference and cavalier treatment for so long and could only wonder that she had not outgrown her girlish adoration of him much sooner.

Perhaps she had . . . and perhaps it had needed the impact of her encounter with Gavin Brice to shatter the crystal cage in which she had been imprisoned. Now, like a newly released bird, she longed to spread her wings still further and to enjoy the freedom of no longer caring for someone who had certainly never cared for her very much. If she must stay with Ritchie because circumstances demanded it, then she would do so — but she was determined to lead her own life to a much greater extent in future. For six years, she had been a docile puppet on a string, allowing herself to be manipulated as her husband wished, much too naive to realize that loving is as much a matter of taking as well as giving . . .

She could feel sorry for Ritchie, of course. All unconsciously she had cheated him . . . attracted by the glamour of his stardom, swept off her feet by his good looks and his attentions, flattered by his evident desire for her, she had fallen headlong in love with love itself rather than with the man — and rushed him into marriage before he could have second thoughts. For the first time, she wondered if Ritchie had married her with high hopes only to be disappointed and disillusioned . . . recalling the years that they had shared in the close intimacy of marriage and yet worlds apart in everything that mattered, Jessica knew that she had failed him just as he had failed her — and all because neither of them had truly loved.

Perhaps his sudden and alarming illness was part of the pattern that shaped their lives . . . perhaps they were being offered a second chance to make something of their marriage. Certainly they seemed closer than they had ever been and she knew that she had a greater understanding of life and love thanks to her brief sojourn at Redvers House . . .

Ritchie soon began to take an interest

in the outside world once more. One morning Jessica brought him a stack of newspapers and, slipping one from the pile, she went to curl up in an armchair by the window. A comfortable silence descended broken only by the rustle of pages or an occasional exchange of comment on a certain piece of news or item of theatrical gossip.

Idly glancing through her newspaper, Jessica was not prepared for the shock of delight that lifted her heart when a certain name leaped out of the page at her . . . but dismay quenched delight as she went on to read that Gavin Brice was often seen in the company of his former fiancée and that neither was denying the suggestion that they were intent on picking up the threads of their earlier romance.

Jessica was stunned . . . and yet there was no reason for her to feel that Gavin had betrayed her. So little had passed between them . . . nothing had been said that gave her the right to resent his renewed interest in Hester

219

Carslake. It had been foolish in the extreme to attach so much importance to the fact that he had admired her enough to want to paint her, that he had generously offered a warm friendliness and a welcome sympathy, that she had appeared to possess some degree of physical attraction for him. A man could want a woman without caring for her, she reminded herself bleakly . . . it had been ridiculously naive to dream that his longing could be born of loving.

He had never spoken of love . . . only of wanting her. He was a man who had desired and won many women. He had offered her nothing more than a brief, careless rapture — and she ought to be thankful that circumstance had prevented her from succumbing to that persuasive charm. His desire for her had been fleeting, merely born of propinquity . . . and she had been pathetically eager to seize on it as evidence of a deeper, more meaningful relationship to come. They had been brought together by chance and he had found her attractive . . . hurt and unhappy and humiliated, she had been very ready to be consoled by the flattery of his interest. Well, that was very human . . . but then she had been stupid enough to fall in love with him — and she was doubly foolish because she was not free to give her heart to any man. Trebly foolish because it had always been obvious that he still cared for Hester . . . the fact that her portrait occupied such a pride of place in his home told its own story, after all.

Deep in her troubled thoughts, she was worlds away from Ritchie. But she was abruptly jerked out of her reverie when he gave a sudden, despairing groan.

"What is it . . . are you in pain?" she asked urgently.

He ignored her, staring down at the photograph and its caption which had caught his attention. His jaw hardened. Suddenly he crumpled the newspaper and tossed it across the room. "Yes,

I'm in pain," he said harshly. "This bloody place gives me a pain! How much longer do I lie here while the world goes on without me?"

Jessica rose and went to him, took his hand and clasped it tightly. "I know it's hard . . . but you must try to be patient, Ritchie," she said soothingly.

He jerked his hand free. "I'm not a patient man . . . you ought to know that! Find that doctor and tell him I'm getting out . . . I'd rather risk another coronary than die of bloody boredom!"

"Oh, Ritchie — do hush!" Jessica exclaimed anxiously. "You aren't supposed to get excited . . . "

"Excited! You have to be joking!" he said mockingly. "I should think there's more going on in the mortuary right now! I can't take any more of this, Jessica . . . there's absolutely no reason why I can't take things easy in my own home."

"You'll be just as bored . . . " she began tentatively, meaning that he would turn to various projects for interest and do too much too soon and she would be powerless to stop him.

"For God's sake, don't argue with me, Jessica!" he snapped. "Find that doctor! I want to talk to him!"

Alarmed by the glitter in his dark eyes, by the scarcely suppressed fury that tensed his words, Jessica hurried from the room — and fortunately ran into the very man that Ritchie was demanding to see.

While the two men discussed the suggestion of Ritchie's discharge on his guarantee that he would live like a vegetable for as long as his medical adviser thought wise, Jessica tidied the room. She bent to pick up the newspaper that had been crumpled and thrown, smoothing it out automatically. Seeing the photograph that had disturbed Ritchie so much, she looked at it intently . . . but it did not immediately occur to her that it could be the cause of her husband's outburst.

It was a photograph of Gavin Brice and Hester Carslake looking tenderly into each other's eyes beneath the words: *Renewed Romance for R.A.* Below was a coy reference to the anticipated announcement of their resumed engagement.

Jessica almost crumpled the offending paper in her turn. Her heart cried an instinctive protest at the implications of that photograph and its accompanying words. She was flooded with bitter resentment for it seemed that Hester, not content with almost wrecking her marriage, had deliberately chosen to reclaim the one man in all the world who really mattered to her.

She had called this woman her friend, she thought bitterly. She had admired her as a charming, attractive person and confided her troubles to her and believed in the sincerity of her sympathy and advice. Who could have known that beneath all the beauty and seeming sweetness of nature lurked a cruel and scheming woman who did not care that others suffered as long as she got what she wanted!

To think that she had felt sorry for her that day when she had failed to see Ritchie! She had believed that Hester was genuinely concerned that Ritchie was ill, that she was genuinely distressed because she was denied the right to be with him at such a critical time. Yet here she was, an incredibly short time later, gazing into another man's eyes and allowing the Press to speculate on their possible marriage! So much for her anxiety about Ritchie and her professed love for him! It seemed to Jessica much more likely that Hester had only used an association with Ritchie as a lever to bring Gavin to the point of resolving the quarrel which had ended their engagement.

Suddenly Jessica was struck by a thought and she turned to look at Ritchie who was carrying his argument with the sheer force of his personality while maintaining a cool calmness that was obviously impressing the medical man. Knowing him so well, Jessica did not doubt that he would win the day . . . but she could not help wondering what had prompted that abrupt impatience with his enforced stay in hospital.

The press photograph could not have escaped his attention. Had it roused him to a sudden determination to get back to a more normal way of life? Had he suddenly realized that his chances of happiness were slipping through his fingers while he lay in a hospital bed cosseted by the wife he had promised to discard? Was it possible that he really cared for Hester despite a careful pretence of indifference?

A man like Ritchie would need a terrific incentive to divorce a wife who had always done her best to please and content him. It would incur the kind of publicity he detested, for one thing . . . for another, he was the type who shrank from unpleasantness and hated to hurt anyone and would do almost anything to win the liking and admiration of those with whom he came into contact. He was a sentimentalist who relied on his charm and personality to get him what he wanted in life . . . until he wanted something very badly and saw it eluding him. Then, driven by circumstances, he could be brutally ruthless . . . as long as he need not stay around to witness the consequences of his actions.

Jessica might have good cause to hate Hester Carslake at the moment but she could not deny that she was the kind of woman who inspired affection and admiration in people without any seeming effort on her part. It would not be so astonishing if Ritchie had fallen under her spell and learned to love at last . . . and it could only be a deep and lasting love that had urged him to end a marriage that suited him so well, to hurt a wife who had nourished his ego with uncritical adoration for so many years.

If she was right then he must be suffering a similar kind of heartache to her own and if Hester and Gavin were to marry then his future would seem as bleak and as unpromising as her own. But they were still married and perhaps they could make something of a shared future if they both had to suffer the frustration and despair of loving someone beyond their reach . . .

13

HESTER was not thinking very clearly when she turned to Gavin during those difficult days of Ritchie's illness. Anxious and depressed, she needed the comfort and consolation that he offered and she did not pause to wonder why he was suddenly so attentive. He had always been a kind and swiftly sympathetic person, generous with his understanding ... no doubt he was still fond of her and it was like him to be on hand when she needed him. They had been friends for a long time before she made the mistake of encouraging him to propose marriage; the subsequent ending of that ridiculous engagement had caused a rift that she had regretted and now she welcomed this renewal of their friendship. It seemed to her that they were on much closer terms than before but it was the warm intimacy of affection and understanding between people who asked nothing more of each other, she told herself comfortably.

She was merely irritated when she saw the first mention in the newspapers of their resumed friendship . . . one or two meetings in public places and the press boys began to speculate, she thought drily. It only emphasized how wise she had been to be discreet in her dealings with Ritchie, sensing that the merest hint of unwelcome publicity would frighten him into breaking off their association.

She was much more than irritated, some days later, when an over-eager reporter dug up an old photograph of herself and Gavin, taken when their previous engagement was at its height, and reprinted it as current with the suggestion that they were about to be married. She was filled with acute alarm. She knew how likely it was that Ritchie would see or hear the ridiculous gossip . . . and it might be all that Jessica needed to convince him that a divorce would be a mistake.

Gavin declared that Jessica was very much in love with her husband. A wife who cared enough to be clever in the handling of the present situation could eradicate another woman from her husband's life quite easily — and the beautiful and usually triumphant Hester was deeply disturbed. For she was also very much in love with Ritchie Conrad and desperately afraid that all the plans they had made together were destined to come to nothing.

She was well aware that in a crisis such as Ritchie had just experienced a man was likely to draw closer to his wife . . . and to suffer all the pangs of an over-active conscience if there was another woman in his life. It was cold comfort for Hester to tell herself that she was more than just 'another woman' and that Ritchie really loved her, really wanted to marry her, and had proved it by discussing divorce with Jessica before his illness. For he had not once asked to see her although he was now well enough to receive visitors. He had not sent her even the briefest of notes or telephoned her . . . and Hester was beginning to believe that this was his way of letting her know that their affair was at an end.

She was hurt and troubled . . . and too proud to approach him for an explanation. So she stayed away, contenting herself with sending gifts and good wishes and waited in vain for some word that would bring reassurance to her anxious heart.

The following day she learned that Ritchie had left the Clinic . . . and mingled with the thankfulness she felt that he was fully recovered was a renewed surge of optimism for the future. Now surely he would soon be in touch with her or else she would hear that an official separation had been announced by the Conrads — and then she would know where she stood.

Ritchie loved her. He would not let her down. She had only to be patient for a little while longer. After all, one would expect Ritchie to be discreet, to guard his reputation very jealously for fear of offending his fickle public . . . and it would certainly tarnish his image if he too quickly discarded the loving wife who had rushed to his side as soon as he had been taken ill.

Privately Hester did not believe that she was a loving wife. It seemed much more likely that a sense of duty and an uncomfortable attack of conscience had brought Jessica to town in such haste. She had not discovered how it happened that Jessica had been at Redvers House but she had her suspicions. Gavin was not a man that one could question on so delicate a subject but questions were scarcely necessary when one recalled his reputation and had gleaned from a remark carelessly uttered that he was working on a portrait of Jessica Conrad. He invariably became emotionally involved with his subjects to some degree.

Their idyll had been brought to a premature end by Ritchie's illness . . . and Hester was inclined to believe that Gavin was relieved and thankful and considered it a timely end. Perhaps he had found Jessica too intense for his taste, too ready to find consolation for an uncaring husband in his arms, too swift to assume that a light-hearted affair must inevitably lead to a permanent and lasting relationship.

Certainly he had not seen Jessica during his stay in town and whenever he referred to her it was always to stress her devotion to her husband and her reluctance to consider divorce. At first Hester had supposed that he was trying to talk her out of the determination to have Ritchie for herself . . . later, she suspected that he was whistling in the dark, fearing that Jessica might turn to him if Ritchie did desert her and trying to assure himself that there never would be a divorce between the Conrads.

Naturally he would not want to marry Jessica, thought Hester confidently. There was only one woman in his life that he would marry . . . and that was herself. She believed that he would never marry if he could not have her — and during those moments of depression when it seemed that all her hopes of a future with Ritchie were doomed to disappointment she sometimes toyed with the idea of becoming Gavin's wife, after all . . .

Gavin knew her moods, knew the way her mind worked and he believed that if he could but judge the right moment she would fall like a ripe plum into his hand. He thought grimly that he would ensure that she had no time to change her mind again . . . and he set about acquiring a special licence Deliberately he fostered her suspicion that Ritchie's desire for her was weakened by the enforced separation . . . and he hammered home his own conviction that Jessica was deeply in love with her husband and would use her present advantage to the full. If he could only whisk Hester out of their path to happiness he did not doubt that Conrad would soon dismiss all thought of divorce and settle down once more with his loving and very loyal wife.

He went down to Redvers House for a few days . . . the exhibition of his work was looming and he had to make the final decision on the canvases he would show. He forced himself to add the finishing touches to Jessica's portrait and survived the agony of longing that consumed him. It was not easy for him to give up all hope of possessing the only woman he had ever truly loved but he knew that there was no hope for him while she remained bound by her feeling for her husband. He must simply accept the inevitable and try to regard those few days with Jessica as an experience which had enriched his life and brought him a new humility, a new understanding.

Rosa sensed the unhappiness which lay behind the effort to seem his usual self and her heart was heavy with sorrow for him. She loved him very much and it seemed a tragedy that the one woman he had sought all his life should be denied to him . . . he scarcely mentioned Jessica but it was obvious that the woman had now gone out of their lives and would not return. It was all very well to argue that he had known from the beginning that Jessica was a married woman . . . the heart did not make that kind of distinction when it gave itself involuntarily.

She could not talk to him about this difficult time in his life but she could offer her affection and her sympathy in a good many ways and she did so. Gavin was touched and grateful and could not refuse to let her help him to marshal and catalogue the canvases he intended to exhibit although he usually preferred to do these things on his own. There was little left to do when Hester telephoned him and sounded so depressed and unhappy that Gavin felt he must promise to go back to town that day . . . and he left Rosa to finish off in the studio, confident that she understood his instructions.

There were no problems . . . until Rosa came across the covered portrait of Jessica, set aside with an air of finality. She had not seen it before and she caught her breath at its magnificence, its pure compassion. Tears rushed to her eyes. This was surely the best thing that Gavin had ever done . . . might prove to be the best that he would ever achieve. But for this canvas alone he would surely be remembered as a great artist . . .

It did not occur to her that he did not mean to show it . . . she labelled and catalogued the canvas, packed it carefully and set it with the others that would be duly collected and taken to the gallery in London where the exhibition was to be held. Then, satisfied with a job well done, she went to telephone to make arrangements for the collection of the canvases . . .

Gavin reached town to find Hester

on the verge of even greater depression and she almost fell on his neck in gratitude that he at least had not deserted her completely.

Knowing that Ritchie was out of hospital, she had scarcely left her flat for fear she should miss his telephone call — but he had not rung her. She had watched and waited for the postman — but there had been no letter. She had swallowed her pride to telephone him — and Jessica had answered, obviously vetting his calls. Yet Hester did not blame her for Ritchie's failure to get in touch with her. If he really cared, he would go to any lengths to see or speak to her at this particular time, she thought bleakly — and so it seemed that he no longer cared . . . if he ever had!

Seeing the sadness that haunted her eyes and the dark shadows that underlined them, noting that she talked too much and too quickly, emptily chattering as though she dreaded a silence that might be invaded by unwelcome thoughts, Gavin knew a surge of compassion. She really was in love with Conrad, he thought wryly — the man must possess some kind of magic to hold a woman captive. The whole world knew how badly he had treated his wife — and yet Jessica apparently adored him still. And here was Hester . . . cool, capable, level-headed Hester . . . head over heels in love with the man and making herself ill with longing for him.

He swiftly suppressed the ardent wish that Conrad felt the same way about Hester — for that would make Jessica very unhappy and his sole purpose in life just now was to ensure her happiness if he could.

Hester poured it all out to him and he listened patiently. When she ran out of words, he said gently: "You ought to go away for a while, Hester . . . it isn't doing you any good to stay here brooding over the whole thing." He smiled at her with sudden warmth. "Come away with me," he said lightly.

"We'll have a few days in Paris and then drive down to the Riviera . . . we can both forget all about Conrad and his wife and remember how much we used to enjoy each other's company in the old days."

She looked at him, unsmiling and not at all tempted. "I couldn't do that," she said soberly. "The press would get hold of it and they've done enough harm as it is." She picked up a day's-old newspaper and tossed it over to him. "I suppose you didn't see this?"

He glanced down at the offending photograph and its headline and raised a faintly amused eyebrow. "But this is old, surely?"

"*We* know that, naturally. But why should anyone else recall seeing it in the papers over a year ago? I imagine the entire population of London believes that we are about to get married!"

He laughed softly. "Is that so terrible?"

"But it isn't true!" she exclaimed

sharply, amazed that he did not realize all the implications of the press gossip and what it could do to her chances of happiness. "We must put a stop to all this nonsense," she went on firmly. "It means that we won't be able to meet so openly for a while but . . . "

He interrupted her, saying quietly: "It doesn't have to be nonsense, Hester . . . we could turn it into fact."

She turned quickly to look at him in surprise.

"Are you serious?" she demanded. "Are you asking me to marry you?"

He smiled at the familiar, characteristic bluntness. "We could make it work, you know," he said, lightly.

"Oh, Gavin — you know the circumstances!" she exclaimed. "How can you possibly expect me to marry you?"

Indeed he knew the circumstances, he thought grimly. She had talked freely and at considerable length of her love for Conrad, the plans they had made together and her fear that his illness had altered everything: he had yet to hear her utter one word of sympathy or concern for the woman who would surely suffer if Conrad persisted in his desire for a divorce. He felt even more determined to protect Jessica from the heartache and humiliation that Hester would so heedlessly thrust upon her . . . and he refused to be deterred by Hester's unflattering reaction to his proposal. He reached for her hand and drew her down beside him on the leather couch.

"I don't *expect* you to marry me — but you can't blame a man for hoping," he said lightly, that attractive smile dawning in his eyes. "I could make you happy, Hester — I know it." He kissed her gently on the lips.

She was perturbed, briefly at a loss. She had come to rely on the fact that their friendship made no emotional demands upon her . . . his proposal was a surprise. She was fond of him, anxious not to hurt him — but she had to make him understand that there was only one man in all the world who could make her happy.

"Perhaps you could . . . if Ritchie didn't exist," she said slowly, ruefully.

He kissed her again and this time his lips lingered, were more demanding, more forceful. "He doesn't exist . . . he's a mere figment of your imagination," he murmured, consciously exuding that physical magnetism which had won him the women he wanted in the past.

He had never found it so difficult to make love to a beautiful woman but his heart was not in the task he had set himself. All his loving, all his longing were centred on one woman and he rather felt that no other woman could ever satisfy the deep primeval need within him that had been awakened by Jessica . . .

"Sometimes I wish that were true," Hester sighed despondently.

Touched by the sadness in her tone, he put both arms about her and drew her close, motivated by a desire to comfort her . . . and she relaxed against him, drawing instinctively on his inner strength. Much more sensitive than he appreciated, she knew that he had no real desire to marry her, that there was no real warmth or meaning behind his kisses or his embrace. She was puzzled. For whatever was prompting him to urge her into marriage it was certainly not an impulse born of loving.

She drew away slightly to study his handsome face but his expression gave nothing away. "Why do you want to marry me, Gavin?" she asked curiously.

He laughed softly. "Why does any man ask a woman to marry him, my sweet?"

"Oh, for a variety of reasons! Never mind — it doesn't really make any difference why you want me. I can't marry you." For one brief, incredible moment she had been tempted. For perhaps he was right . . . perhaps she ought to marry him and try to put Ritchie out of her life. But the very thought of losing him irrevocably had caused her heart to cry out in instinctive protest. She could not do it! She could not give him up! "I'm sorry, Gavin," she said firmly. "I have to believe that Ritchie still loves me, still wants me . . . and that when he's well again . . ."

He was suddenly white with anger. He released her abruptly, rose to his feet and strode to the window, hands thrust deep into his trouser pockets to still their trembling. "And Jessica?" he demanded harshly.

"What about Jessica?" There was a hint of defiance in her swift retort.

"Don't you care at all what you are doing to her? Can't you spare an ounce of compassion for her feelings?"

Her chin tilted abruptly. "Why should I, Gavin? She's had him for six years — now it's my turn! He doesn't love her and she must know it — if she had any pride at all she would never have waited to be told that he didn't want her!"

Gavin regarded her coldly. "You are

living proof that a woman in love has no pride."

She shrugged. "I wouldn't hang on a man's neck once he'd made it obvious that I meant nothing to him."

"Hasn't Conrad made it very obvious that his wife means more to him than you do? You bewitched the poor devil, that's all — but that was enough to break his wife's heart. Now she has a second chance — and you can afford to be generous. Give them the chance to make something of their marriage — as they will with you out of the way. For God's sake, do the decent thing and allow them to be happy!"

His words were a revelation. His concern, his depth of emotion, could only mean that he loved Jessica Conrad . . . and loved her enough to marry another woman if such a step could further her happiness. Hester conceded that Ritchie would probably stay with his wife if she were to walk out of his life for good. But she was not prepared to sacrifice even the smallest chance of her own happiness on such a quixotic altar. Gavin was trying to be noble . . . but there was nothing noble in four people being miserable because they were tied to the wrong partners.

She shook her head. "I'm not giving him up unless that's the way he wants it," she said stubbornly. "And I'll hear it from his own lips before I believe it!

I'm sorry if Jessica gets hurt — but I expect you'll be around to kiss her better! That's the way you want it, isn't it?"

Gavin refused to quarrel with her but it took an effort to control his temper. Instead he took his leave of her . . . and they parted on far from amicable terms. But while he was furious with Hester he realized that she was sincere in her love for Conrad and he supposed it was only natural for her to fight tooth and nail for what she wanted. She believed that Conrad wanted her, too — and that only his illness combined with his wife's determination to stand in their way was preventing them from being together.

Honesty compelled him to admit that if he thought that Jessica cared for him he would go to any lengths to bring about an end to her present marriage in order to secure the happiness that they could know together . . .

14

RITCHIE paced the room restlessly, a scowl marring his handsome features. He felt perfectly fit again and he grew more and more impatient with the restrictions that both his doctor and his wife still placed upon him.

He had soon discovered that leaving hospital for the luxurious flat overlooking the park had not brought a swift solution to the problem of Jessica and the future.

She nursed him with absolute devotion — and it had become increasingly more difficult to remind her that he wanted his freedom. She had taken it for granted that his illness had eradicated his desire for a divorce whereas it had impressed him with a much greater need to be free of a meaningless marriage. The traumatic experience he had undergone had served to emphasize that life was too short to be spent with the wrong woman — and his life might well prove to be shorter than that of many men. He had wasted too many years but he had been granted a glimpse of what life could really mean with a woman he loved and who loved him.

He was determined to know more of that happiness. But how . . . without destroying the wife who undeniably cared for him? The wife who had generously forgiven the heartache he had caused her and could not do enough for him. She scarcely left him for more than ten minutes at a time, sought to tempt his appetite with every known dish, restricted his visitors so that he should not be overtired or over-excited, constantly reminded him that he must not think of working again for a very long time — and almost convinced him that he was doomed to invalidism for the rest of his life. She never allowed him to forget that he had been very ill and might be so again — and it was nerve-wracking.

He was constantly aware of irritation and exasperation with the wife who tried so hard to please and only succeeded in infuriating him. She smothered him with affection and solicitude — and how could he guess that she was motivated by deep feelings of guilt because she was never free of love and longing for another man?

For his part, he ached for Hester and the cool serenity that soothed and stimulated him at the same time . . . the longing for her was gradually becoming unbearable. Since he had left the Clinic the gifts and the notes had ceased and she had not been in touch with him. He understood, of course . . . she would make no further move while Jessica remained with him and he allowed the world to suppose that their marriage was mended. Hester was a proud woman who would ask nothing that he was not prepared to give — and give freely.

The newspaper gossip had angered

and upset him but it had been quickly forgotten. He did not believe that Hester would desert him. He needed to believe that one day soon they would be together with all their problems solved . . .

Jessica looked up from the letter she was writing as he crossed the room from window to fireplace for the tenth time in as many minutes. He was very restless and she knew that it was one of his bad days. It was natural that he should vent his unhappiness and frustrations on her. He never mentioned Hester, never admitted his need for her — but Jessica was sure that he was troubled by the woman's desertion of him for Gavin. She thought how ironic it was they should have a common cause for despair. She was very sorry for him and so she tried to be patient, to endure his moods, while her own heart ached and she wondered if the fierce need for Gavin would ever cease to torment her.

She put away the writing materials

and closed the bureau. Rising, she went to Ritchie and linked her hand lightly in his arm. "You seem bored. What would you like to do today?" she asked brightly, smiling up at him.

He looked down at her coldly. "Do I have freedom of choice?" he asked bitterly.

"It's such a lovely day," she said, indicating the wide blue sky and the bright sunshine with a sweeping gesture of her hand, ignoring the harshness of his tone. "We could walk in the park . . . I'm sure it would do you good to go out for a little while."

"It would do me a great deal of good to kick up my heels and paint the town red — but I suppose you'd veto that!"

"Soon you may paint the town red, white and blue — and I'll help you," she promised gaily. "But just now you have to take things easily, remember!"

"Do you allow me to forget?" he demanded impatiently. "If I'm to be perpetually wrapped in cotton wool I might as well be dead . . . because this isn't living!"

Her face clouded. "I'll get my coat," she said quietly. "You'll feel better for some fresh air."

As she went from the room, Ritchie slammed a fist into the palm of his other hand in frustrated fury. She would not even quarrel with him to relieve the utter boredom of his existence, he thought angrily . . .

It was a lovely day but he was in no mood to appreciate its beauty. He walked dutifully in the park with Jessica by his side but there was no enjoyment to be found in his surroundings or his companion. In his mood of longing and frustration it seemed to him that every woman he saw reminded him achingly of Hester and her cool elegance, her tantalizing beauty, her exciting promise of a new and wonderful world. And he was still tied to this woman by his side! It was intolerable! He could not go on much longer without insisting on his freedom — come what may!

He turned abruptly. "Let's go back . . . I've had enough!"

"Are you tired?" Jessica asked anxiously. He looked pale and strained. It was obviously going to be a long time before he was really fit. She stifled a sigh. It was so much more difficult than she had expected. There were moments when she felt that he wished her anywhere but with him . . . and moments when she longed desperately for the peace and happiness she had found at Redvers House and wondered if she would ever be happy again.

"No, I'm not tired," he returned brusquely. "Will you stop fussing over me like a hen with one chick?" She did not answer. He looked down at her, suddenly contrite. She was doing her best and all he ever did was to use her as a whipping-boy! He reached for her hand and drew it beneath his arm and when she glanced at him in surprise he smiled at her with some trace of his former boyish charm. "I'm sorry,

Jessica — I don't really mean to be so beastly to you."

"It just comes naturally, I suppose," she retorted with an attempt at flippancy.

"Let's say it has become a habit not to consider your feelings," he amended wryly.

Her eyes widened. "There's honesty for you," she said lightly.

"If we had been more honest with each other we might have had a better marriage," he said soberly.

"If we had been more honest with each other we might never have married at all," Jessica said drily. She was suddenly weary of all this life that was no life at all. It was all a futile pretence . . . he cared for her as little as she cared for him. Some degree of affection might remain but it was not enough on which to found their future. It was better to separate, to make new lives for themselves — and it was what he wanted, she knew. He did not need her at all. She took a deep breath — and plunged. "We shouldn't have married, Ritchie. I adored you — but I didn't really want to marry you. I just didn't have the courage to say so! I think I suspected you weren't the god I imagined you to be but just an ordinary man who'd turn out to be more selfish than most . . . but I didn't want it proved!" She smiled at him, a tender little smile that took the sting from her words. "And you only wanted to sleep with me, Ritchie. You dressed it up in all sorts of finery but basically you wanted me and had to have me — even if it meant marrying me! I was a disappointment to you — in bed and out of it! We were both disappointed — but we couldn't be honest and . . . "

Finding his voice at last, he interrupted her roughly "What is all this? Why the post-mortem?"

She seized on his words. "You see! You accept that our marriage is as dead as a door-nail! It is, isn't it, Ritchie?"

He was astonished by the seemingly sudden *volte-face* but thankful for it.

Relief gradually seeped through his entire being. "If that's the way you want it," he said slowly, looking down at her incredulously.

She nodded. "I want a divorce, Ritchie," she said quietly, firmly.

He checked his stride. Oblivious to their surroundings, the curious glances that they attracted, he turned her to face him with both hands on her slim shoulders. He studied her face intently. "Are you saying this because . . . well, because of what happened before I went to Cyprus? Are you doing this for my sake?"

"No . . . for my own!" she retorted swiftly. "I want to be free!"

He was not convinced. "Are you sure? Aren't you just being generous because I told you that I want to marry someone else?"

She shook her head, smiling. "I'm being selfish, Ritchie. You see, I found out that I can be independent of you — that I can be happier without you, in fact! I'm not being cruel," she added hastily. "Just honest!"

"Happier without me . . . " he echoed slowly. "Happier with someone else . . . is that what you mean?"

Faint colour stole into her face. "I don't know . . . perhaps — one day!"

"Why didn't you tell me?" he demanded fiercely.

"I thought you needed me," she said simply.

His hands tightened abruptly on her shoulders. "I think I do, Jessica," he said tautly.

"Oh, Ritchie . . . !" she exclaimed in laughing reproach "That's so like you! You don't want me — but no one else must have me!"

He grinned ruefully. "Stupid, isn't it?" He released her and they walked on once more. "Do I know the man?" he asked curiously.

She bit her lip. "There isn't . . . I mean — I haven't any plans, Ritchie. I just want to be free."

He nodded in understanding. "Suddenly I couldn't bear to think of you with another man . . . but that's force of habit, I suppose. I don't grudge you happiness, Jessica. You've been my wife for a long time. It hasn't been a bad marriage, has it?"

"I think we both knew there had to be something better if only we had the courage to go out and look for it," she said gently.

"I never wanted to hurt you," he told her quietly.

She smiled at him in warm affection. "Do you know what was wrong with our marriage, Ritchie?" she asked levelly. "We liked each other too much — and we didn't love enough."

Leaving the park, they continued to discuss an amicable divorce as they made their way back to the flat. They turned into Bond Street, deep in discussion, closer to an understanding than they had been for a very long time. Suddenly Ritchie halted. He had seen Hester stepping out of a taxi and his heart had stumbled. So had his feet. It seemed an eternity since he had seen the woman he loved . . . it was all he could do to stop himself from calling her name as she paid off the taxi and turned to enter a famous gallery.

Jessica had not noticed the taxi or its occupant. "What is it?" she asked urgently, thinking he felt ill.

He looked at her blankly. Then he pulled himself together. "I saw someone I knew," he said carelessly. Then he indicated the gallery which was advertising an exhibition of the work of Gavin Brice, R.A. "That might be interesting . . . let's go in and have a look. He's a fine artist, you know."

"Now . . . ?" Jessica was taken aback.

"Why not?" He took her arm and guided her across the road.

With a pounding heart, she followed him into the building and instinctively she looked for Gavin among the press of people. There was no sign of him and she knew a swift disappointment.

Ritchie moved cursorily from canvas to canvas, his gaze sweeping the crowd for a glimpse of Hester — and when he finally saw her, he strode swiftly to her side, forgetting everything but his need to know the touch of her hand, to hear her voice, to snatch a few precious moments with her. It was a very public declaration of his feelings . . . and so was the look in Hester's eyes as she greeted him.

Abandoned, Jessica stood still . . . and when she saw the radiance in Hester's beautiful face, saw how joyously their hands touched and clung, saw how oblivious they were to everything but each other in that moment, she was happy for them . . . but as she turned to leave and saw Gavin a little distance from her, intently regarding the same scene, her heart was swiftly touched with sadness for him.

Impulsively she went over to him and laid her hand tentatively on his sleeve. "I'm sorry," she said gently.

He smiled down at her, accepting her presence without question although he had been unaware of it until she came to his side. "Jessica . . . " he said, covering her slim hand with his own. He studied the lovely face that had haunted him continually. "How are you?" he asked gently.

She ached for the tenderness she heard in his voice. She had longed for the comforting strength of his nearness and the reassurance that she found in the mere touch of his hand. Her heart swelled with love for him — and suddenly she knew that they were meant to be together till the end of time. She did not understand it . . . she just knew that all her unhappiness was at an end and that her future lay with this man.

"Oh, Gavin," she said unsteadily. "I have missed you." She smiled up at him through a mist of tears. "I was so afraid you meant to marry Hester."

Her words and the unmistakable wealth of emotion behind them were entirely unexpected . . . but he welcomed this revelation of her love for him with a glad heart. Heedless of the curious throng, he bent his head to touch her lips with his own . . . and in that moment he claimed her as his lasting love. Then he drew her towards the large canvas that had excited so much interest among the art critics. "Let me show you the only woman I mean to marry," he said, smiling . . . and Jessica paused before the magnificent portrait with its symbolic meaning.

She was no longer that lost and lonely girl, scarcely knowing what she sought. She had found what she needed so much . . . a lasting home for her loving heart that was no crystal cage to shatter in a moment but a secure haven built on the rock of true love.

THE END